THE UNEXPECTED PATH

ALSO BY BARBARA HINSKE

Available at Amazon in Print, Audio, and for Kindle

The Rosemont Series

Coming to Rosemont

Weaving the Strands

Uncovering Secrets

Drawing Close

Bringing Them Home

Shelving Doubts

Restoring What Was Lost

No Matter How Far

When Dreams There Be

Novellas

The Night Train

The Christmas Club (adapted

for The Hallmark Channel, 2019)

Paws & Pastries

Sweets & Treats

Snowflakes, Cupcakes & Kittens (coming 2023)

Workout Wishes & Valentine Kisses

Wishes of Home

Novels in the Guiding Emily Series

CONNECT WITH BARBARA HINSKE ONLINE

Sign up for her newsletter at **BarbaraHinske.com**
 Goodreads.com/BarbaraHinske
 Facebook.com/BHinske
 Instagram/barbarahinskeauthor
 TikTok.com/BarbaraHinske
 Pinterest.com/BarbaraHinske
 Twitter.com/BarbaraHinske
 Search for **Barbara Hinske on YouTube**
 bhinske@gmail.com

THE UNEXPECTED PATH

BOOK TWO OF THE GUIDING EMILY SERIES

BARBARA HINSKE

CASA DEL NORTHERN PUBLISHING

ISBN-13: 978-1-7349249-3-0

LCCN: 2021907178

Casa del Northern Publishing

Phoenix, Arizona

To Daniel Nevarez, for living your life with such admirable courage and unrelenting optimism, to Julie Rock for your continuing insight and unwavering support, and to Cynthia Woods and Biscuit for contributing Biscuit's admirable example to the story. Your input has been invaluable and I'm deeply grateful.

CHAPTER 1

*E*mily Main pushed a thick plait of her long auburn hair off her face and groped around on her nightstand for her phone. "Mom? What time is it?"

"It's six fifteen. Did I wake you?"

"It's fine. I get up at six thirty to take Garth out to do his business." Emily sat up and threw her legs over the side of the bed. "What's up? Are we still on for today?"

"That's just it. We'll have to change our plans."

Emily's heart sank. She'd been so busy with work these past months that most of her things in the studio apartment were still in boxes. Martha was supposed to come into the city to help her organize—they'd planned to make a weekend of it. More than Martha's organizing prowess, Emily craved the comfort of her mother's presence.

Unwanted tears stung her eyes. The months she'd spent in her new studio apartment hadn't been an unmitigated success. She hadn't slept well, waking to every new floorboard squeak or rattling pipe in the old building. She'd bashed her shins countless times on unopened boxes and fumbled to find items that hadn't, as of yet, been assigned to their permanent homes.

Emily knew, in her mind, that all of these things would get sorted out in time. In her heart, however, she just wanted her mother.

Garth picked up his head and looked at Emily. "What's ..." Emily took a deep breath to steady her voice. "Why?"

"Do you remember me telling you that Irene's been having pain

in her hips?"

"She's been complaining of that for as long as she's lived next door to you." Emily didn't intend her words to sound as sharp as they did.

"I've been telling her she needed to see her doctor about it. Anyway, she fell last night when she was getting ready for bed. Zoe heard her and came over to get me."

"That's awful." Emily pictured how scared nine-year-old Zoe must have been. "What did you do?"

"I tried to help her up, but we couldn't budge her—she was in too much pain. I called the paramedics, and they took her to the hospital."

"I'm so sorry for Irene—and Zoe. Have you heard any more?"

Garth got out of bed and came to Emily's side, resting his muzzle on her knee. She brought her hand to the top of his head and rubbed behind his ears.

"Irene just called. She's broken her hip, and they're going to do surgery tomorrow to replace it."

"I'm sorry she has to go through this, but I'll bet she'll feel much better with a new hip."

"That's what I think. Anyway, I've got Zoe and her miniature schnauzer—you remember Sabrina—staying with me while Irene's

in the hospital."

"I figured as much."

"That's why I can't come down to San Francisco. I'm sorry, Em. I was looking forward to spending the whole weekend together."

"I was looking forward to spending time with you, too, Mom." Emily controlled the quiver in her voice. "We'll do it as soon as

Zoe can go back home to Irene. I'm perfectly capable of organizing my apartment on my own," she said, not feeling the conviction

she spoke with.

"You know how much I love doing that."

"It's one of your core strengths, that's for sure. You can help me fine-tune things when you do come." Emily searched with her toes for her slippers and slid her feet into them. "How's Zoe doing with all of this? After she lost her parents in that car accident several years ago, I know she's extremely attached to her grandmother."

"She was petrified last night, but the emergency room doctor that updated us on Irene's condition did a fantastic job of explaining things to Zoe over the phone and reassuring her that Irene should make a full recovery."

"That's a relief. I hate to think of Zoe suffering any more loss."

"Thank goodness she has that miniature schnauzer. She took Sabrina out as soon as she got off the phone, and then they both went to bed. They're still asleep."

"What do you have planned today? Will you go to the hospital?"

"Irene thinks it'll be better if Zoe doesn't see her until Monday after she's had her surgery. I thought we could go to the store to buy craft supplies and make a nice card for Irene. Maybe go to a movie." Martha sighed. "Any suggestions?"

"Well … why don't the two of you come into the city today? Are you too tired to drive in?"

"No. Not at all."

"You could both help me get settled. I'm not trying to inconvenience you—I can handle it all myself—but Zoe is endlessly interested in the adaptations I have to make. I think she'll have fun, and it'll take her mind off of her grandmother."

"You know what? You're exactly right. That's a great idea."

"You'll have to leave Sabrina at home. This apartment is small, and I don't know how she and Garth would do, being cooped up together."

"Of course. She'll be fine." Martha was silent for a beat. "Em—what would you think about Zoe spending the weekend with you? She'd jump at the chance. Is that too much of an imposition?"

"Genius idea! I'd love it!"

Martha could hear the smile in Emily's voice. "I'm going to let Zoe sleep in. I'll text you when we're on our way."

"Perfect. I've got to take Garth out and feed him. Then I'll pull myself together. No rush. I'm happy that I'll get to spend time with my two favorite gals."

"We'll probably be there by mid-morning. I'll stay until after lunch; then I'll come back here to take care of Sabrina. I'll drive in on Sunday afternoon to collect Zoe."

"We'll do Sunday night supper, the three of us."

"You're positive you don't mind? It's not too much trouble?"

Emily leaped to her feet and snatched her robe from the foot of the bed. "Positive." She grasped the guide dog harness from its place on the chair next to the bed and slipped it effortlessly over Garth's head. "See you soon. I need to take care of my best guy here."

Martha chuckled. "Give him a belly rub for me."

CHAPTER 2

I looked back over my shoulder at Emily. It was a sunny, crisp morning—beautiful to be outside. She led me behind our building, to the spot where I know to relieve myself. I wagged my tail in appreciation and did my business, but I really didn't have to go.

Emily rested her hand on my back, gauging my body position.

She could tell that she wouldn't need to clean up after me with one

of those little plastic bags she carried in the zippered pouch that's clipped to my leash.

"Good boy," she said as she picked up her coffee cup from

the ledge where she'd set it and took a long, slow sip. Her second cup of the morning.

I was all in favor of Emily slowing down a bit. What did they call it? Stopping to smell the roses? I was pretty sure we were going to be late to work.

6

I turned my nose in the direction we should be going and gave a slight tug on my harness.

"Garth, down," Emily said.

I obeyed. Oh, boy. This meant we were going to be here for a while. I blew out a breath and put my chin on my paws. I'd tried to tell her we were going to be late for work.

Emily tilted her face to the sky and smiled into the sun.

I wagged my tail—I couldn't help myself. Her hair shone like a new penny, and her skin was luminous. My Emily is the most beautiful woman I've ever seen.

Footsteps approached from around the corner, crunching across the gravel. I knew who it would be and shifted my eyes toward the newcomer. Emily followed suit shortly after I did. Her hearing wasn't as good as mine, but it was getting better.

My tail began to wag again as Dhruv came into view.

"Good morning," he said.

"The same to you," Emily replied, sounding chipper. "Looks like we're finally going to have a beautiful Saturday."

"Rain's not predicted until Monday night," he replied. "Our first clear weekend in months."

"It's about time. What do you plan to do today?" Emily asked. "Will you take your dogs to the dog park?"

"This afternoon, I will—or at least I'll take them for a walk. I'm going to install more lighting in your apartment this morning."

Emily swiveled her head to Dhruv. "What are you talking about? I don't need lighting."

"I read that you do. You can see light and shadow, right?"

"Yes."

"At work, you can see the lights in the elevator that line the floor."

"I can. How did you know that?"

"I've watched you in the elevator. You took your cane and explored the area where the floor meets the wall. There are rope lights outlining the floor of the elevator."

Emily took a step back.

I lifted my head off of my paws. Whatever they were talking about had surprised her.

"I did. I wanted to know what I was seeing. I can't believe you noticed that."

A grin spread across Dhruv's face. "I thought so. I went online and ordered enough rope lights to outline your apartment. That way, you won't ever run into the wall when you're moving around with your cane or," he pointed in my direction, "this guy."

"I don't know what to say," Emily said. "That's so thoughtful of you."

"Do you think it'll be helpful?'

Emily nodded. "I do. And I'll pay you back."

"My uncle said he'll cover it as part of building maintenance. I'm going to put them in this morning. That's why I came looking for you."

"That's incredibly nice of both of you."

"It won't take long. I just staple them in place."

"Then let's get going," Emily said, grasping my harness. "Garth, home," she said.

I was on my feet in an instant. In no time, we were at the door to our apartment. The boxes of lights were stacked up in the hallway.

Emily unlocked the door, and we entered our apartment.

Dhruv brought in a stack of boxes and an oddly shaped red thing that made a whirring noise. He set the red "drill"—at least that's what I think he called it—on the floor and shut the door behind him.

"Before I start, can I—" Dhruv stopped abruptly.

"Can you give Garth a treat?" Emily asked.

I looked between them, suddenly interested in this exchange.

"You are a dog softie, aren't you, Dhruv? Yes—you can give him a treat—but just one."

Dhruv fished in his pocket, and my heart skipped when I saw the cylindrical orange object laying on the open palm he extended to me. A Crunchy Cheeto—my very favorite snack.

I extended my tongue, and that most perfect of all culinary delights was gone in an instant.

"But it had better be a dog treat, Dhruv. Not one of those snack foods you love so much."

Dhruv looked at me, and our eyes met. We stared at each other, and I knew we were thinking the same thing. What was done was done. There was no point in telling Emily.

CHAPTER 3

$\mathcal{E}$mily inserted a coffee pod into the appropriate slot and placed a paper cup under the spout before pushing the start button. The machine hummed as the heating element kicked on. Emily could just make out the bright green light as it raced in a circle while the coffee dispensed into the cup. When she could no longer hear coffee dripping, she grasped the cup and moved cautiously to where Dhruv stood, unboxing the rope lights.

"Here you go," she said, holding the cup out to him. "I remember from work that you drink it black, right?"

"Yep—that's right. Thank you," Dhruv said, taking the cup. "What're all those boxes and envelopes lined up against the other wall?"

"Kitchen supplies for the blind," Emily replied. "I got a list of what I'd need from the foundation and ordered all of it online."

"I thought you didn't know how to cook? You always said that you could find anything you wanted to eat at any time of day or night in this city—that there was no point in cooking."

"I had to learn a little bit about cooking in my program at the foundation. It was kind of fun. I'll probably still order in most of the time but decided I might as well equip my kitchen —in case I ever do want to cook."

"That's a lot of stuff to unbox and put away."

"My mother and Zoe are coming over this morning to help me with it. I've pulled all of my receipts, and I'm going to sit down now with my computer to double-check that I've received everything."

"When I'm done with these lights, can I help open the packages?"

"Don't you have other things you need to do?"

"No."

"Well … then … yes. That would be helpful."

"I'll take all the cardboard and trash out to the dumpster, too."

Emily smiled at him. "That's above and beyond, Dhruv."

Dhruv turned away quickly and picked up a string of lights.

Garth, who had up until this point been watching the exchange like he was secretly hoping for another treat, retreated to his bed in the corner of the studio, next to Emily's bed.

Emily clicked on the inventory she'd prepared and listened as her screen reader voiced the list:

Smart oven

Long oven mitts

Oven rack protector guards

Three talking thermometers

Talking food scale

Braille measuring cups and spoons

Double spatula

Wooden spoons

Bowl scrapers

Vegetable chopper

Lettuce knife

Peeler

Pizza cutter

Cut-resistant gloves

Colored cutting boards

Boil-over disc

Locking-lid pasta pan

Can opener

Beeping liquid level indicator

Braille labeling tape

Assorted peel-and-stick locator dots

Talking PENfriend

Braille UNO cards

That was everything they'd recommended. It seemed like a lot of equipment. She wondered if her mother—a prolific cook —had all of this stuff. She'd ordered the card game on a whim to play with Zoe in case the fourth-grader ever visited her. Emily was glad she'd added it to her shopping cart. That would give her something fun to do with Zoe tonight.

Emily crossed to the counter and found the sink. She filled a glass with water and caught an open box with her elbow, sending its contents tumbling to the floor. She flinched as she heard the sounds of plastic containers hitting and skittering across the kitchen tiles.

Emily dropped to her knees and picked up one of the items, cursing under her breath. "It's my makeup, Garth," she said softly. "I forgot that I put it there." She unscrewed a lid and gingerly tapped her fingertip against the broken fragments of powdered eye shade. "This is worthless," she said. "I can't believe I did this. I knew I stashed that box there last night." She rocked back on her heels and dragged her free hand through her hair. "I'm still struggling to put on makeup so that I don't look like a clown. I'll make a huge mess trying to deal with this."

She continued to gather up the remaining jars and makeup containers, confirming that all of the powders had shattered. Her hand brushed against the bottom of the glass cylinder that held her liquid foundation. The glass hadn't shattered. Maybe she hadn't broken everything. Her hand traced the bottle to the lid and found it cracked and oozing a pool of thick liquid makeup. Nope—she'd ruined it all. Emily pulled the trash can from under the kitchen sink and jammed all of the ruined items into it.

Dhruv's question broke her out of her funk. "Can you make sense of what you're hearing? That text-to-speech program reads incredibly fast. I didn't understand a word of it. The one you use at work is slower."

"I've learned to understand it perfectly. I've set the speed slower at work because it's reading me complex lines of computer coding. I can listen to everything else much faster than I could read it."

"That sounds efficient."

"It is. I get through my emails at least twice as fast as I used to."

"I wonder if I could learn to do that."

"Of course you could. Our work computers have text-to-speech programs built into them. Just turn it on, and you'll soon find yourself increasing the speed setting. Listening is also less fatiguing than leaning into a computer monitor all day." Emily sat up straight. "I'll help you set it up if you'd like."

"That'd be great. I've finished putting the lights around the baseboards. It may be too bright in here right now for you to see them, but I'm hoping you'll notice them at night."

"I'm sure I will. I'm grateful, Dhruv, for everything you've done for me, but you can stop worrying about me. I can manage on my own."

He turned to the mound of packages. "Let's get started on these. What's in this large box?"

Emily shook her head. Subtle hints were lost on him. "It's my smart oven. It's a microwave, convection oven, air fryer, and warmer—all in one. It connects to a smart speaker so that you can control it with a voice-activated intelligent personal assistant."

"You mean, like Alexa?" Dhruv opened the box with his pocketknife.

"Exactly. It's the latest thing."

"Do you know how to use this?" He pulled the appliance out of the box.

"I'm learning," Emily replied. "I can't wait to see what my mom thinks of it. If she likes it, I'm going to order one for her as a thank you."

"Where do you want me to put it?"

"Is there room on the kitchen counter?"

"Barely," Dhruv said, putting the oven where she'd requested. "It's to the left of the refrigerator. The instruction booklet is on the counter next to it."

"Perfect. There's supposed to be a braille display for the keypad. Can you find it?"

"It's right here. Want me to put it in place?"

"Yes."

"Done. Now what?"

"Can you open the rest of the packages and tell me what's inside?"

"You bet. Just tell me where everything goes. I'll keep the

instruction booklets with each item. You don't need to worry about that."

"I know that you're very conscientious, Dhruv. Maybe we can get it all unpacked before Mom and Zoe get here."

Dhruv had already opened the next package. "Vegetable chopper."

"On the kitchen counter. Don't worry if things get stacked up. Mom and Zoe will help me label and put everything in the drawers and cupboards. The only things I already have here are dishes, glassware, and silverware that were wedding presents."

***

"Hello, Dhruv." Martha walked into Emily's apartment and leaned in to give the man a quick peck on the cheek. "How nice to see you."

"Remember me?" Zoe asked. "I'm Emily's best friend, Zoe."

"I remember," he said.

"What're you doing here?" Zoe asked.

"I was helping Emily."

"He's been a godsend," Emily said, stepping to the door. "Wait'll you see. He's saved us so much time unboxing all of my new kitchen gadgets and appliances."

Dhruv picked up the smart oven box filled with the trash he'd collected and slipped out the door without another word.

"Did I make him mad?" Zoe asked. "He left without a goodbye."

"No, honey," Emily said. "Dhruv sometimes gets anxious in social situations."

Zoe nodded. "There are autistic kids in my class who are like that. Is that how it is with Dhruv?"

"Exactly," Emily said.

Zoe stepped to Emily and put her arms around her waist, burying her face against Emily.

Emily hugged her close. "Are you upset about your grandmother?"

The little girl's head bobbed against Emily's rib cage.

"Irene's going to be fine. People break hips all the time, and doctors have been doing surgery to replace hips for years. She'll be back to normal soon. Better than normal."

"You can count on it," Martha chimed in. "She'll be home before you know it."

"Let's tackle all of this stuff that Dhruv and I just unpacked. Since I've never really cooked before, maybe you can decide where everything goes, Mom."

"I'd love to," Martha replied.

"Zoe can help me label things."

"Okay." Zoe dropped her arms from Emily's waist. She was ready to get started. "Like what?"

"For starters, I'd like you to apply graduated raised dots to the stove knobs and the oven controls. The smallest dot is for low, and the largest dot is for high on the stove, and we'll use the smallest dot for 250 degrees on the oven and go up to broil. I have six different-sized dots. I'll tell you where to put them."

"Cool!" Zoe cried.

"Here they are," Martha said from near the counter, handing Zoe a package of self-adhesive dots. "Is this the new smart oven I've heard so much about?"

"It is, indeed."

"Wow. I can't wait to hear what you think of it. If it's as good as they say it is, I might have to get one for my kitchen, too."

Emily smiled.

"Let's get started," Emily said. "I'll make labels using my braille tape labeler, and Zoe, you can peel off the backing and attach them. We can break for lunch in about an hour, and I'll take us all to the café at Nordstrom. How does that sound?"

"I'd love that," Martha said. They hadn't been back to their favorite lunch spot since Emily's riding accident. Martha hated to admit it, but she still felt Emily's British husband was mostly to blame. Connor had pressured her daughter into a horseback ride—for a honeymoon photo—even though he knew a minor fall could cause Emily's weakened retinas to detach, which was exactly what happened. Emily was forced into permanent blindness after subsequent surgeries had failed, and Martha had to watch her daughter fall into a deep depression that kept Emily from enjoying nearly anything that resembled her former life. Hearing her daughter say she wanted to go to the Nordstrom café warmed Martha's heart. Her Emily was officially back.

"Mom?"

Martha shook the thoughts from her mind. "I'd love to go."

"What's a Nordstrom?" Zoe asked.

Emily laughed. "You'll love it. It's a department store but it also has a restaurant inside. You can get any food you want, and their desserts are to die for. We'll have one at lunch and bring some home for dinner."

"Yeah!" Zoe said.

"I also need to stop by the makeup counter," Emily said. "I knocked my entire makeup collection onto the floor, and everything broke into a zillion pieces. I have to replace all of it. I'm such an idiot."

"You're not an idiot. Accidents happen," Martha said. "Besides, it's fun to get new makeup. I got a makeover before your wedding, and I love what they recommended for me."

"They did a nice job for you," Emily agreed.

"I still get compliments on it," Martha said. "When Irene

looked at the wedding photos, she told me it made me look years younger."

"All right—I'm game. Let's do it," Emily said.

"Let's get cracking!" Martha said. "I'll drop you girls back here after we're done, and then I'll head home to let Sabrina out."

CHAPTER 4

"The line to order is still out the door," Martha said as she, Zoe, Emily, and Garth approached the café inside the department store. The buzz of conversation from the groups of shoppers in line filled the air.

Emily double-tapped her smartwatch and listened to the time. "It's only one thirty," she said. "I'm not surprised. Lunch hour is later on Saturdays. Based on the noise level in here, I'm guessing the store is busy."

"It is," Martha said. "Would you and Zoe like to grab us a table, and I can get our food?"

"I think we need to see what they have to offer—especially the desserts. Right, Zoe?"

"I've never been to a fancy cafeteria like this one," Zoe said. "I'd like to see it."

"It's bustling." Martha turned to Emily. "Are you okay with this? Will it ..."

"Trigger a panic attack?" Emily asked. "Crowded public places aren't my favorite, but I'm with the two of you—and

Garth. I'll be fine. Besides, I haven't had one of their famous salmon niçoise salads since before my accident. I'm hungry for one."

Their group inched forward as they talked.

"The line is moving," Martha said. "We'll have plenty of time to eat and get your new makeup before I have to head for home."

"You've both been such a big help," Emily said. "I'm very grateful."

"I thought you had a husband," Zoe broke in. "Connor. Why isn't he helping you?"

"Connor lives in Tokyo," Emily said.

"Why don't you live there with him?"

"We ... we're not together right now."

"So, are you getting a divorce?"

"That's a lot of questions, honey," Emily stammered. "I don't know."

"How come you don't know?"

"Connor and I need to decide."

"When will you do that?"

Emily sighed in exasperation. "We have to talk about it."

"Here we are," Martha said as they reached the serving line. "Zoe—grab a tray and put it on this wire shelf. You pick out what you want to eat, and they'll hand it to you to put on your tray."

Zoe did as Martha instructed and began looking at the sandwiches and salads tilted for display behind a glass shield. "They have pizza," she said. "Can I get that?"

"Whatever you want. My treat," Emily said. "And don't forget to pick out a dessert, one for now and one to take home. They're at the end of the line, by the cashier. Keep your eye peeled for them. You get to choose for us."

Martha leaned in and spoke quietly to Emily. "Now's not the time or place, but I think Zoe's got a good point. You've got to talk to Connor and figure out what the two of you are doing about your marriage."

Emily jerked her face away from her mother. "I'm not ready to deal with my marriage, Mom. I've got enough to think about with returning to my job and learning to live independently."

"I know, Em. And you're doing a fantastic job with all of it." Martha pushed her tray along. A man behind the counter asked them for their order.

"We'll have a margarita pizza, a salmon niçoise salad, and ..." Emily turned to her mother.

"Make that two of those salads," Martha said.

The man handed them a ticket and told them that they would bring the salads and pizza to their table.

Garth continued to lead Emily forward to the cashier.

Zoe picked out a lemon square, a berry tart, and two chocolate chunk cookies to take home.

Emily took her credit card out of its designated slot in her purse and handed it to the cashier.

The cashier returned it to Emily with a pen and a credit card slip.

Emily felt for the countertop and placed the slip on it. She positioned the pen in her hand and spoke to Zoe. "Can you read me the amount?

Zoe complied.

"Place your finger at the line that says 'tip.'"

Zoe put her finger on the credit card slip.

Emily wrote down an amount. "Now move your finger down to the total so I can fill that in and then to the signature line."

21

When they were done, Emily held out the signed slip and pen to the cashier.

Martha led them to an open table along the wall.

"You were very helpful, Zoe," Martha said.

"Now I know how to use a credit card," Zoe said. "I'll bet nobody else in my class knows how."

Emily sat down, and Garth settled himself at her feet under the table. "I'll bet you know all kinds of things that your classmates don't know."

"I have another question," Zoe said.

"Shoot," Emily said as the waiter brought their entrees and beverages.

"Your silverware is on the left side of your plate," he told Emily as he put her salad on the table, "and your drink is at two o'clock."

Emily smiled and thanked him.

"Do blind people always have to wear black?"

Martha and Emily both laughed.

"No. Why would you ask that?"

"Because you always wear black."

"My wardrobe has been mostly black for years," Emily said. "I guess I've never been interested in clothes, and it was just easier that way. Everything matched."

"That's good because now you wouldn't be able to see what colors you had on. If Connor was with you, he could tell you, but you live alone."

"I could still wear any colors I wanted to. Blind people sew tiny braille markers into their clothes that tell them what color they are."

"That's so interesting," Martha said.

"I'm lucky because I can still see bright colors," Emily said. She turned to Zoe. "I can tell that you've got on a pink T-shirt."

"I do! I don't like black," Zoe said. "If I was blind, I'd get a whole bunch of those braille markers."

"You know, it's probably time I put some color into my wardrobe," Emily said. "I'm going to order a set of those markers. Maybe the two of you can help me pick out some new tops."

"That'll be so cool," Zoe said. "You need a pink T-shirt, like mine."

CHAPTER 5

*C*onnor Harrington III lifted the silver-framed photo of his wife from his now-empty desktop in Tokyo. The candid image of Emily, throwing her head back and laughing at a remark he'd made out of frame, made his heart soar as much now as it had the day he'd taken it. He tore his eyes from the picture and wrapped it carefully in bubble wrap before placing it into his carry-on suitcase. He wasn't going to take the chance that the airline might lose it.

Emily's photo was the first thing he'd unpacked when he'd arrived in Japan to open the initial Asian field office for his Fortune 500 company. The job had been a plumb assignment: It was everything he'd worked for and dreamed of since he'd gotten his graduate degree more than ten years ago and started working for the company. He'd made the new office an unparalleled success, with revenues that were triple those projected in the business plan.

A knock on his door brought Connor out of his reverie. He turned to face his boss, who had flown in earlier in the week to assure that the transition to Connor's successor went smoothly.

"I knew you were coming back," Roger Foley said, leaning against the doorframe. He pointed to the picture, now nestled in Connor's suitcase. "You'd never leave that behind."

"You're right," Connor said in his crisp British English. "It's the only personal item I keep in my office, and I'm never going to part with it." He cleared his throat. "At least, I hope I'm not."

"You've done a stellar job for us here, Connor. I was planning to promote you to a director role."

Connor felt his stomach contract. Less than a year ago, he would have jumped at the opportunity. He and Emily had both talked about living and working internationally. They'd been eager to experience everything the world had to offer.

"I understand—and respect—the reasons you want to return to San Francisco."

"Thank you, Roger. I've got to see if Emily and I can make our marriage work. I don't know if I was wrong to take this job while she was learning how to live with her blindness," he placed his palms on the desktop and leaned over it, arms stiff and his face tilted down, "but I can't continue to be away from her."

"Losing her eyesight in a freak riding accident on your honeymoon was nothing short of tragic. You both had a lot to adjust to."

Connor nodded.

"I'm happy that she wants to give your marriage a try."

Connor inhaled sharply. Emily hadn't answered any of his calls, emails, or texts—for months. Would she want to have another go at their marriage? Was he foolishly giving up his dream job—and a huge promotion—on the baseless hope that Emily would even talk to him?

"I have to do this," Connor said, as much to himself as to his boss. "I can't go through my life wondering what might have been." He zipped his suitcase shut.

"The position in San Francisco is a lateral move. It's the best the company could offer on such short notice."

"I understand, and I appreciate your making a spot for me."

"I think you'll be bored with it, Connor. It'll pale compared to the excitement and challenges you've handled here."

"There are far worse things than being bored." *Like losing your soul mate and love of your life*, he thought.

Roger extended his hand to Connor. "I wish you the very best in all of this, Connor. Keep me posted."

The two men shook hands. "Thank you, Roger. I'm grateful for every opportunity you've given me and all of your support."

"If new positions under my umbrella become available, I'd like to reach out to you."

"I'm grateful, sir, but I think my future will be tied to San Francisco."

"I'll contact you, nonetheless. You can always say no." Roger stepped aside. "And now, I think you've got a plane to catch."

CHAPTER 6

The young woman behind the makeup counter noticed the auburn-haired woman with the black lab guide dog, flanked by an older woman and a young girl, step off the escalator. Her pulse quickened as the older woman turned them toward her. Karen stepped around her co-worker and met Emily as she reached the counter.

"Good afternoon, ladies," Karen said. "Can I help you?"

"I need to replace these," Emily said, pulling a handful of makeup containers out of her purse and spreading them on the counter. A narrow, cylindrical jar began to roll toward the edge of the counter. Karen snatched it before it fell to the floor.

"I see," Karen said, bending over the items. She picked up an eyeshadow and turned it over to read the label on the bottom.

"We don't carry all of these brands, but I can help you find something similar." She looked at Emily. "If you don't mind me asking, are these for you?"

"Yes."

"Have you used these products for a while?"

"Since before I … I lost my eyesight."

"I was wondering how you distinguished one product from another. The eyeshadows are from the same cosmetic line and the containers feel the same. You haven't labeled these jars in any way. Can you see well enough to distinguish them from each other?"

"I have a pinhole of vision in my left eye, but it's very time-consuming to try to find the right one that way. I've just learned how to apply makeup as a blind person. We're going to mark everything when we get home with a device that attaches a talking label."

"A PENfriend. My sister uses one to identify her makeup—and a lot of other things."

"Is your sister visually impaired?"

"Yes—she has keratoconus. She applies her makeup by touch—just like I'll bet you've learned to do. She has the most gorgeous makeup I've ever seen. Hers looks better than anyone working here in the makeup department."

"That's saying something, isn't it?" Martha interjected.

"That's encouraging," Emily said. "I live alone and don't want to go out of the house looking like a clown. I've been hesitant to start wearing it again."

"You don't need much," Karen said. "Your skin is flawless, but you'll need a foundation with sunscreen and blush. Your eyes are striking. Neutral shadows, eyeliner, and mascara are all you'll need." She reached over and gently lifted Emily's hair away from her face. "Your eyebrows are fine as they are."

"I have my hairstylist color them when I go in for a cut."

"That's what I do, too," Karen said. "You'll only need a few products for your eyes and complexion. Add in a tinted lip gloss, and you're done."

"Does your sister use any special products?" Zoe asked. "Like, are there special ones for blind people?"

"That's a great question," Karen replied. "There are products that are easier to apply and more forgiving of errors. We've worked out what works best for her in every category."

"Can you suggest the right colors for me in all of those products?" Emily asked.

"Sort of a mini-makeover," Martha suggested.

"Do you have time?" Emily asked. "Should I make an appointment and come back another day?"

"I have all the time you need," Karen said. "I'm going to bring one of our tall stools over to you so you can sit. I'll apply the product to one eye, and you can do the other. I want to make sure you're happy with what I recommend. Your ..." she turned to Martha.

"Mother," Martha supplied, "and our friend Zoe."

"Mother and Zoe can watch and tell us what they think. I'll be selecting products from several cosmetic lines so the packaging will feel different for each product. The eyeliner I'm going to give you is very creamy and glides effortlessly along the lash line. The mascara won't clump. You'll leave here feeling confident that you can apply your makeup like a pro."

CHAPTER 7

I lay down on the cool marble floor, with my hindquarters under the tall stool where Emily perched, my front half leaning toward the left. A jazzy, formless sort of music that I didn't care for played softly in the background. The new woman named Karen, whose lips were an unnatural shade of deep red, hovered on Emily's right side. Karen was poking and prodding at Emily's face with all sorts of sticks and wands, but Emily didn't seem to mind. If it was okay with my Emily, it was okay with me.

Whatever this place was, it had a lot of interesting smells. Upstairs, in the restaurant, food smells had been bold and forthcoming. Sweet and spicy, with unmistakable jolts of coffee. Nothing challenging to identify.

This area was a different story. I lifted my nose and flared my nostrils. I picked out flowery scents, together with an antiseptic smell coming from a spray bottle that Karen frequently squirted on the sticks she was using.

An overspray drifted down to me, and I sneezed loudly. I

glanced up at Karen, hoping she would take the hint and watch where she was spraying that stuff.

I was lowering my head to my paws when I caught a whiff of a scent that caused me to bring my head back up. I'd smelled this before—a subtle, layered blend of rose, ylang-ylang, jasmine, lily of the valley, and iris over a warm, woody base of vetiver, sandalwood, vanilla, amber, and patchouli.

I wracked my brain, and a snippet of memory came to me. That scent had been in the condo where Emily and I had spent a night. She'd called it … "Chanel No. 5."

A petite, pretty young woman with hair the color of a yellow lab came into view, carrying the scent towards us.

CHAPTER 8

*G*ina Roberts folded the garment bag over her arm and stopped at the end of the makeup counter, behind where Emily sat on the stool.

Martha lifted her chin and looked over the top of Emily's head at the young woman she'd loved like a second daughter. Their eyes locked. She'd never have believed that Gina could betray Emily, but something had happened between Connor and Emily's best friend that day Emily had found them together in his condo.

Gina began to blink rapidly, and a tear escaped the corner of one eye, making its way onto her cheek. Gina brushed it away with her free hand.

Martha made the first move. "Hello, Gina," she said quietly, stepping around Emily and reaching out a hand, awkwardly grasping Gina's elbow.

"Hi," Gina said.

Emily spun towards them.

"Hi, Em," Gina said, her voice choked with emotion.

"Gina," Emily said quietly. She stood.

"You … you look great," Gina said, then instantly regretted it. "I mean …"

"I'm getting a makeover," Emily continued, smoothing over Gina's awkwardness. "I graduated from the school for the blind's basic training and learned to do my makeup again."

Gina stepped closer. "It looks fabulous, Em. You've never needed much, with that perfect complexion and to-die-for hair color."

Zoe leaned against Emily, tugging on her sleeve.

"Where are my manners?" Emily put her arm around Zoe's shoulders. "Gina, this is my very good friend, Zoe."

"You're the girl that lives next door to Martha, aren't you?"

Zoe nodded.

"I've heard a lot about you," Gina continued. "Like how smart you are and how helpful … what a good friend … you've been to Emily." Her voice cracked on the word "friend."

"Gina was my very best friend," Emily said in strained tones. "We've been friends since we were both your age."

"Have you met Garth?" Zoe asked. "He's Emily's guide. I talked her into getting him."

"He's a beauty," Gina said. "He's got his harness on, so I know he's working. I'll ask to greet him another time."

"Thank you," Emily said. "I'm surprised you know the etiquette around guide dogs."

"I've learned a whole lot about … about how the visually impaired do things," Gina said. "I wanted to know what you'd be facing. I'm thrilled that you have a guide dog. It looks to me like you've taken control of your life, Em. I always knew you would." She brushed away more tears.

Emily knew her friend was crying. She cleared her throat. "What are you doing here today?"

"I just picked up a gown from the alterations department. They had to shorten the hem about six inches."

"I don't remember you ever buying a dress that didn't need to be shortened," Emily said. "Did you get this gown for a special occasion?"

"I'm going to the black-tie gala to support the ballet."

"Ohhh … that sounds fancy. You've always loved the ballet. Who are you going with?"

"Craig Johnson. He's … we've been dating for a while."

Emily inhaled deeply, and they stood in silence. "I'm happy for you," she said quietly.

"Thanks, Em. He's a great guy."

"Sounds like the two of you have a lot to catch up on," Martha said.

Gina kept her gaze fixed on Emily's face.

Emily smiled. "I think tomorrow is your birthday," she said.

"You remembered!"

"Of course I remembered."

The phone in Gina's purse pinged.

"That's my reminder," Gina said. "I need to be at my hairdresser in twenty minutes. I'm having my makeup done and getting an updo." She reached over and touched Emily's hand. "I'd better get going. I'm so glad I ran into you … all of you."

Emily squeezed Gina's hand. "Have a wonderful time tonight. And a very happy birthday tomorrow."

"Thank you. And if you'd like to catch up, please call me. I … love you, and I miss you, Em."

Martha leaned into Gina and brushed her cheek with a kiss before the young woman stepped into the crowd of shoppers and was gone.

***

Martha pulled to the curb outside of Emily's apartment building. "Are you positive you can manage?" Her voice trailed off as she cut her eyes to the backseat where Zoe sat, looking out the window and engrossed in the sights and sounds of San Francisco.

"We'll be fine," Emily said. "We got the kitchen labeled and set up before we left for lunch. You've both been so helpful. It feels like it's about to rain, so I thought we'd stay in the rest of the day.

We can label my new makeup and order a pizza for dinner. We'll hang out on the sofa and watch movies or play UNO tonight. How does that sound, Zoe?"

"Great!" came the reply from the backseat. "I've got the shopping bag with all your new makeup right here. I'll be really careful with it."

"I know you will be, sweetie," Martha said. "I'll pick you up at dinnertime tomorrow. In fact, why don't I bring dinner to you? I'd love to try that new smart oven of yours. I'll be here at four to cook dinner. Would that be all right?"

"I figured you'd be itching to get your hands on it. We'd love that."

"How about I do some grocery shopping for you? Get you stocked up for the week?"

"I can do that for myself, Mom."

"I know, but it'll make me feel useful." She reached across the console and put her hand on top of her daughter's. "I've got a couple of additional kitchen utensils that I'll bring you, too. I have duplicates at home. Now that you're going to cook, you'll need all the equipment."

"You've never met a kitchen gadget you didn't like, have you?" Emily chuckled and squeezed her mother's hand. "Thank you, that would be helpful."

"Okay, you two. I'd better get home. Poor Sabrina is probably dying to get outside to do her business. I'll see you both tomorrow afternoon. Have fun."

"Tell Sabrina—and my gramma—that I love them."

"Will do," Martha said. "Don't worry—they're both going to be fine."

Emily and Zoe got out of the car and headed toward the building, with Garth leading the way.

CHAPTER 9

Zoe and I sat on the floor, next to the coffee table.

"It's all spread out," Zoe said.

"Great," Emily said, sinking to her knees next to us.

Small round containers covered the coffee table. Even with the lids screwed on tight, I could detect their sweet, floral scents. Those containers held makeup.

"You've got the pen and the programmable stickers, too?" Emily asked.

"Yep. I read the directions, and I know how to use them, too."

"You are a brilliant girl," Emily said, finding Zoe's back and rubbing it. "I'll feel each item. I want to see if I remember what it is, based on feel."

"Okay. For every one you get wrong, I get to stay up an extra ten minutes."

"Deal." Emily moved her hand from Zoe's back to mine and gave me a quick rub. "I don't want to get in trouble with your grand-mother," Emily said. "I know she's strict about bedtime. I'd better get this right." She picked up a round, thin container. The package contained a small, raised bump that released the lid when pushed. "This is my overall, peachy shadow."

Zoe took it from her. "Right!"

I wasn't surprised. My Emily is so smart.

Zoe removed a dot from a ribbon of similar dots and stuck it to the top of the eye shadow. She put the PENfriend into Emily's hand and positioned one end over the dot. "Press the button and speak into the other end of the pen."

"Peach shadow," Emily said.

"That should have recorded on the dot. Try it," Zoe said.

Emily felt the dot on top of the shadow and placed the pen on top of it. She pressed a different button on the side of the pen and heard her own voice saying, "Peach shadow."

"Cool!" Zoe exclaimed.

Emily set the labeled container to one side and picked up a similarly round container. "This one has a smaller circumference and is taller," Emily said. "This is the taupey-brown shadow that goes in my eye crease."

"Right again!"

I looked between them as they worked their way through all of her purchases. Emily's confidence was growing with each correct answer, and the cloud of heaviness that had hung over Zoe since she'd arrived that morning was continuing to dissipate.

"You have a great memory," Zoe said.

"Did you notice how carefully Karen went through everything with me at the store? She was so helpful. I can't believe we were lucky enough to find such a knowledgeable salesperson."

I agreed with Emily. That Karen was nice.

"I focused on everything she was saying. That's why I remembered when I got home. It's easier to remember things you focus on."

"Then why did we label everything?"

"I might forget—and it was good practice, learning to use the PENfriend."

"It's really cool. We can label the groceries that your mom brings in tomorrow if you want."

"Great idea. I can always use the app on my phone to identify things based on their barcodes, but it'll be faster to have them labeled."

"You got all the makeup right."

I could tell that Zoe was disappointed.

"I did, but you've been such a big help to me that I think you should get to stay up later tonight. It's Saturday night, after all."

"Really?"

"How about another half hour?"

"That'd be awesome."

Emily retrieved her phone from the coffee table and tapped the screen twice to hear the time. "It's almost six. Time to order pizza." She searched for the app she used to order food from local restaurants and held the phone out to Zoe. We ordered food almost every night.

"Scroll to see what you'd like. You get to choose the toppings."

Emily and Zoe listened as the phone recited, "Pepperoni, spicy Italian sausage, extra cheese."

I was praying for Italian sausage. Emily never gave me people food. That would be breaking the rules. Just filling the apartment with the aroma of the spicy sausage would be a treat for me.

"Have you ordered food on your grandmother's phone?"

"No. She doesn't know how to do that."

"You should learn. You can finalize our order. I'm going to feed Garth."

My ears perked up. I liked this turn of events.

"But ..."

"I'll be right here if you have questions. We're both learning new things today."

I followed Emily into the kitchen. She found the rolling bin that contained my food. My bowl was right on top, where she'd left it.

I panted noisily by her side.

"Garth, sit," she commanded.

She reached over and touched my back, confirming what she

already knew.

Of course I was sitting patiently.

She placed two level scoops of the delicious dry food in my bowl and put it on the floor.

"Okay—break," she said.

I gave my full attention to my supper.

"All done!" Zoe called from the living room. "It says it'll be here in an hour."

"What do you want to do until then? We can watch TV."

"How do you do that?"

"I have the audio description enabled on all my streaming services so I can listen to dialogue and descriptions of action. It's not much different than listening to an audiobook."

I finished my kibble and took a big drink of the cool water that she always kept available for me.

Emily sat down next to Zoe and picked up the remote, clicking it into the space in front of her.

The television came on.

"Can I try it?" Zoe asked.

Emily handed her the remote, and Zoe zoomed through the apps on the screen.

"There's a dog show on now," Zoe said. "Can we watch it until the pizza gets here?"

I perked up my ears and positioned myself at the end of the sofa with a good view of the television.

"I'd love that," Emily said.

"I'll bet Garth will like it, too," Zoe said. "If he were there, he'd win."

I brushed my tail along the floor. This girl Zoe was very discerning.

"Best in show, for sure," Emily said, leaning over and massaging my ears in the way she knew I loved.

"After dinner, can we play UNO? You said you bought cards?"

"A braille version. I remembered that you and your grandmother love to play UNO."

"We always play on Saturday night before bedtime," Zoe said in a small voice.

"And you'll be playing with her again, very soon. She's going to come through this surgery just fine."

"You really think so?"

"I do."

"You're not worried?"

"The only thing I'm concerned about is you beating the pants off me. I haven't played UNO for years."

"Well ... I'm pretty good. I can't promise anything."

Emily laughed. "You're not going to let the poor blind girl win?"

"Nope. I don't think you'd want that."

"You're right. Just treat me like anyone else—that's the best thing you can do for me."

I worked myself into position between them. My belly was full, and my two favorite humans were happy and having fun. I couldn't ask for more.

CHAPTER 10

*C*raig Johnson took Gina's hand and led them to the line of guests waiting to have their pictures taken. The lobby of the theater that was home to the ballet company was filled with women wearing jewel-toned or sequined gowns set off by a sea of men in black tuxedos and bright white shirts. The can lights in the high ceiling lent an elevated brightness to the scene. A wall of floor-to-ceiling calla lilies served as the photo station backdrop. A placard proclaimed that proceeds from all portraits would benefit the ballet company.

Craig leaned over and put his lips close to her ear. "You're the most beautiful woman here. I definitely want to have a photo of us." He moved to kiss her, and she pulled her chin away.

"You'll mess up my lipstick before we have our picture taken, silly." She smiled up at him. "And thank you, but this place is packed, so you couldn't possibly know that."

Craig straightened to his full height of six foot six and purposefully studied the crowd before bending down to her again. "I've now seen everyone in attendance, and I stand by my statement. You are the most beautiful—by a country mile. That dress matches your eyes. What do they call that color?"

"Sapphire," Gina replied. She touched the lapel of his tuxedo and ran her hand along it. "You're incredibly handsome, yourself."

"I haven't worn a tuxedo since my senior prom," he said. "I felt incredibly out of place then, but I'm sort of liking it now."

"It suits you. Very George Clooney."

"I guess that's a good thing?"

"It certainly is."

"Then we should get dressed up and go out like this more often. Maybe I'll buy myself a tuxedo."

"You could do that. You'd be able to wear it for years. I, on the other hand, would have to buy a whole wardrobe of formal dresses."

They inched forward in the line.

"Would that be a hardship? I thought women loved to buy fancy dresses."

"I do enjoy shopping. And today, when I picked up my dress —I have to get everything I buy hemmed—I ran into an old friend that I haven't seen for ages." She turned her head aside, suddenly overcome by emotion. She blinked rapidly.

"Are you … crying?" He brushed a tear from her cheek with his thumb.

"She's a friend I really love, but we had a falling out."

"How'd it go when you saw her this afternoon?"

"Fine. Awkward at first, but it was nice." Gina took a deep breath. "She even remembered that my birthday is tomorrow."

"What? Whose birthday?"

"Stop." Gina punched him playfully in the arm. "I know you remembered. You've been teasing me about the fact that I'll be a year older than you. It'll only be until your birthday next month."

He brought her hand to his lips and kissed her knuckles before tucking her hand in the crook of his elbow. "What's your friend's name?"

"Emily. She's the one that lost her eyesight on her honeymoon."

"You've mentioned her. That must have been devastating."

"It was. She had so much to cope with. But Em is an incredible gal. I've always known she could conquer anything. When I ran into her, she was at the makeup counter, getting a makeover. She's also got a guide dog now."

"Maybe she needed time to adjust to her blindness; maybe you can resume your friendship."

"It's more complicated than that," Gina said. "She thinks I did something awful."

"I can't imagine that. You're too good of a person. It must be some sort of misunderstanding."

Gina lowered her face to the floor.

"Would you like to tell me about it?"

Gina lifted her eyes to his.

"Whatever it is, you can tell me."

She stared into eyes that held nothing but love and compassion.

"Okay, lovebirds," the photographer called to them. "It's your turn."

Craig and Gina swung to face him.

"Sorry—I wasn't paying attention," Craig said to the man.

"You only had eyes for this lovely lady. And I can see why. Step right over here." He positioned Craig on the left with Gina on his right. "This will be a stunning portrait against that backdrop. You'll want to frame a copy to show your kids."

Craig tightened his arm around Gina, and she blushed.

The photographer gave them the usual instructions to look toward the hand he held up and smile. He snapped four pictures before handing Craig a card with a website and order number on it. "You'll be able to order prints by the end of tonight's performance. I'll take hundreds of photos by the time I'm done tonight. I can promise you—yours will be among the absolute best."

Craig thanked the man and tucked the card into his breast pocket. "We'll order copies over dessert later."

The lights in the lobby blinked off and on.

"That's our cue—it's time to take our seats," Gina said.

The auditorium doors were flung open by ushers in black pants, white shirts, and red vests with gold embroidery.

"Our seats are through the doors on the left side." She began to make her way across the lobby when Craig pulled her to one side. He put his arm around her waist and stooped. His face was level with hers.

"Let's take a selfie," he said, holding his phone up.

"Great idea." She pressed her cheek against his and smiled.

Craig took three photos. "Maybe you can even send one to Emily."

Gina swallowed hard. That's exactly what she would have done in the old days—before Connor's drunken, meaningless kiss had broken her best friend's heart and torn their friendship to pieces.

They shoved their way into the swarm of patrons and found their seats.

Craig opened his photos and passed his phone to her. "Air-Drop the ones you want to your phone."

She selected the best photo. If she could have one wish for her birthday, it would be for Emily to forgive her and for their friendship to be renewed. If she heard from Emily tomorrow—on her birthday—she'd send the photo. Gina handed the phone back to Craig and leaned in to kiss him.

"I thought you didn't want to ruin your lipstick," he whispered when they were done.

"I couldn't resist you any longer." Gina patted his arm as the lights went down and the curtain rose.

CHAPTER 11

*E*mily opened her eyes. The room was brighter than it usually was when she woke on weekdays. She listened carefully. It must be later than six o'clock. Garth was on his bed, next to hers, but his breathing was quiet and regular, not the deep buzzing inhales and intermittent cheeps he emitted when asleep.

"You need to go outside, boy?"

She reached out a hand, and he put his muzzle into it, brushing her palm with his cold, wet nose.

Emily pushed herself into a standing position and put on the clothes she left at the foot of the bed for her early morning forays to let Garth do his business. She put him in his harness, and they made their way to the door. She retrieved her keys from their hook and then turned back. "Just a sec, Garth."

She moved to the sofa and reached out to find the sleeping form of her young houseguest. She ran her hand along Zoe's back to her shoulder and patted it gently. "Zoe?"

Zoe stirred, then bolted to her feet. "Gramma ... has something happened to her?"

"No, honey, everything's fine. I'm taking Garth downstairs to do his business. I didn't want you to wake up and find me gone. I'll be right back."

"Oh ... okay."

"Come lock the door behind me," Emily said. "I have my key."

Emily and Zoe went to the door, where Garth waited patiently.

"Why don't you think about what you want to do today? We've finished getting my apartment labeled, so we can do anything you'd like. It's supposed to be a sunny day." Emily and Garth stepped out the door.

Zoe pulled on her bathrobe and went into the kitchen. She found the pods of coffee in a wire basket on the counter and placed one in the coffee maker like she'd seen Martha do the previous day. She put a mug under the spout and pressed the button on top. When Emily came back with Garth, Zoe would have a cup of coffee waiting for her.

The humming of the machine stopped as the lock clicked, and Emily and Garth stepped inside. Emily hung her keys on their hook. "Is that coffee I smell?"

Zoe hopped from foot to foot. "Yep. I made it for you."

"You clever girl! Thank you!"

"I watched your mom make it so I could do it for you."

Emily crossed to the girl and gave her a big hug. "You're the best." She wrapped her fingers around the cup and took a sip before feeling for the counter and putting it down. "I need to feed Garth. He's been very patient while the two of us slept in." Emily found his food bowl with her toe, located his kibble, and scooped.

Garth sat in front of his bowl.

"Good boy," Emily praised. "Break!" she said, and Garth dug into his breakfast.

"I'll give him fresh water," Zoe said.

"Have you thought about what you want to do today?"

"Not really. I dunno."

"How would you like to meet up at the park with a friend of mine from the foundation? And her guide dog?"

"That'd be neat!"

"She called me while I was outside with Garth. She's in the city today and wanted to see if we could get together. We've got an hour until we need to leave. Let's get breakfast and pull ourselves together."

"I'll get the cereal out. I know where it is."

"Perfect. I'll shower now while you eat. Pour me a bowl, will you?"

"I'll be quick. I didn't get dirty yesterday, but Gramma always says to take a shower, anyway."

Emily was smiling as she headed for the bathroom.

CHAPTER 12

The three of us were going out. I was wearing my green harness that told the world I was performing the specialized work that I'd trained for: I was guiding my Emily.

I glanced over my shoulder at Zoe. I wasn't an expert on children, but I was pretty sure Zoe was one. She looked to be about the age of the little boy in my puppy raiser family. Zoe was small, like Alex, and she had a little voice. The only thing that gave me pause was that Zoe's heart was sad and heavy like Emily's was at times. Zoe didn't have a child's heart.

The sun was almost straight overhead. The air was cool, but I was starting to get warm. I opened my mouth and let my tongue hang out. We were stepping out at a brisk pace. I loved it when we didn't have to stop for curbs or street crossings—when we could just move seamlessly together. Zoe was skipping to keep up with us, and she had a smile on her face.

I returned my gaze to the path in front of us. This Zoe was

feeling better. We'd gone no more than another twenty steps when Zoe said something to Emily. Her voice was excited.

"Left, left," Emily said.

I turned as directed and took us on an asphalt path through a set of concrete pilasters on either side of the path. A wide swath of green grass lay directly ahead. The sounds of someone kicking a ball came from my far left.

Emily stopped, and I stood in place, hoping we'd continue to the grass. I loved the feel of those soft blades under my paws.

"There's a woman on a bench with a dog wearing a harness like Garth's!" Zoe cried.

I looked at the bench that Zoe was pointing to, and my heart soared. There was my friend Biscuit! She was on duty, of course, with her person—a nice woman named Stephanie. My Emily and Stephanie had become friends at the foundation, and so had Biscuit and I. Seeing her would be better than walking on grass.

I waited patiently for Emily to command me "right, right" before I guided us to our friends. The humans exchanged excited greetings while Biscuit and I were more restrained. We both were, after all, still working. We bumped noses like we used to do in the hallway at the foundation and settled at our respective person's feet. I knew she was as excited to see me as I was to see her.

Our people sat on the bench and talked. Biscuit and I both lay down and put our heads on our paws. The concrete under the bench felt cool against my chest. I closed my eyelids and went into what I liked to think of as my screensaver mode. I wasn't sleeping—I was merely preserving my energy.

CHAPTER 13

"*I*'m so glad to meet you, Zoe," Stephanie Wolf said, pushing a wind-blown strand of her chin-length blond bob off of her face. Emily talked about you all the time at school." She scooted over. "Here,

sit with me."

Garth and Biscuit exchanged a glance and touched noses, then settled in to wait.

"Hey," Zoe cried. "The dogs said hi to each other."

"They became acquainted when Stephanie and I were both studying at the foundation. Did they touch noses?"

"Yes."

Emily laughed. "That's what they used to do. Seems like they formed a friendship—just like Stephanie and I did."

"I guess they haven't forgotten each other," Stephanie said.

"Just like we haven't," Emily replied. "I'm so glad you called me. I've been meaning to get in touch with you since I graduated and went back to work."

"No worries," Stephanie said. "I know how busy it can be,

getting back to your normal life. I heard that you're continuing your braille training."

"I am. I'm working virtually, one-on-one, with a braille coach to learn grade 2 braille and Nemeth braille."

"That's awesome. You took to braille right away—I remember that. And with your line of work—all that technical stuff—you should know Nemeth. As for me, I never learned anything above basic arithmetic, even when I was sighted. I've finished grade 2 braille, and that's all I need."

"What brings you into the city?"

"I'm thinking of taking a teaching job here," Stephanie replied. "There's an opening in a fourth-grade class in the same school that I attended as a kid. It was always my dream to teach there before I lost my sight. I thought that would never happen when I became blind, but they've offered me the job!"

Emily reached across Zoe and found her friend's hand and squeezed it. "I'm thrilled for you!"

"That's really neat," Zoe said.

"I think Emily told me you're in fourth grade, Zoe. How would you feel about having a blind teacher?"

"It'd be cool," Zoe said. "I'd learn a whole lot about how people can do things in different ways."

"Emily said you were very wise," Stephanie smiled.

Zoe grinned. "Thanks," she murmured.

"You said you were 'thinking of taking' the job. What's holding you back?" Emily asked.

"I wanted to come into the city to see if I would be comfortable here—to test my orientation and mobility skills. I've been with my parents in the suburbs since I lost my sight. I need to move out and live like a grown-up again, but I'm scared. I know you're here on your own, so I wanted to see how you're doing."

"You're going to be fine," Emily said. "Just give yourself

time to adjust. The foundation will send an orientation and mobility specialist with you to help you figure out your route to work, the grocery, the bank, and other usual places. And neither of us are alone; I have Garth, and you have Biscuit."

"You think I can do this?"

"I know you can. It's easy to live in this city. There's public transportation everywhere, and the drivers and operators are trained to help people with disabilities."

"That's what I understand."

They sat silently for a moment and listened.

"Do you hear all of that traffic noise? This city is always busy. Noise is a visually impaired person's friend. You can always tell which direction the traffic is coming from. I've heard that it's harder to navigate on quiet suburban streets, especially if you can't feel the sun on your face to tell you where east and west are."

"That's true," Stephanie said.

"And I'm in the city, so we can get together for coffee. I'm even learning to cook. I'll have you over for dinner."

"I'd like that." Stephanie inhaled slowly. "I really want this job."

"Then take it."

"I will. I just needed that extra bit of confidence."

"When would you start?"

"In thirty days. I'll call and accept tomorrow, and then I need to find a place to live. I'm familiar with the area, but I had sight then."

"Where's the school located?"

Stephanie gave Emily the cross streets.

"That's near where I live! My office is there, too. You'll find it very accessible."

"What are the chances of that? We're going to be neighbors. If I can find a place. Is it pricey?"

"I've got a studio, and it's perfect for me. I think you'd be able to afford something like that. Why don't you come by, and I'll show it to you?"

"That would be wonderful. Can I come next weekend?"

"How about Saturday morning? An uncle of one of my employees owns the building where I live. I'll ask if they have any units available or if they have any recommendations about other properties."

"I'd appreciate that," Stephanie said.

Zoe sat quietly between them, swinging her legs back and forth under the bench. A mother pushing a stroller called to a small boy who had darted too far ahead of her.

"And now, I think someone needs to be rewarded for her patience," Stephanie said. "Thank you for letting me intrude on your time with Emily, Zoe."

"It's okay," Zoe said. "You were worried about stuff."

"I was, and now I feel so much better. While I waited for you, I Googled and found a wonderful diner specializing in ice cream desserts. I think all fourth graders like ice cream, don't they?"

"I do," Zoe said.

"I'd like to treat us all to lunch," Stephanie said. "I've got the walking directions all cued up on my phone."

"That's an offer I can't resist," Emily said. "Fourth graders aren't the only ones who like ice cream. Lead the way, Stephanie."

CHAPTER 14

I opened my eyes and quickly got to my feet when Emily pulled on my harness. The sun was bright, and I blinked several times.

"Follow," she commanded, and we set off after Biscuit and her person. I liked that we were going somewhere with them.

We'd no sooner gotten going at a good clip when Biscuit and Stephanie walked through a doorway into a long, narrow room filled with round tables and metal chairs. A woman wearing a white apron greeted us and took us to a table toward the back. I lifted my nose in the air and sniffed. Bacon, coffee, and the yeasty smell of warm bread. We were in a restaurant.

The table was barely large enough for three people. Space underneath it was at a premium. I allowed Biscuit to settle herself before I found a spot for myself. I didn't want to crowd her.

Our people chatted away in happy tones as servers in blue jeans and tennis shoes went back and forth to our table, finally bringing plates full of food that I thought smelled delectable.

I lowered my head to my paws. Biscuit and I both knew that begging for food was bad form. A well-trained guide simply didn't do it. I kept my eyes open just in case a scrap of food fell to the floor. Food on the floor was, in my humble opinion, fair game.

Biscuit was the first to see it. Her head came up sharply, and I followed her gaze.

A small hand had inserted itself under the table, holding a french fry between her thumb and pointer finger.

Biscuit looked at me and slid her eyes to the delicious morsel.

I raised my eyebrows in response. I knew that Zoe was breaking the rules. We should say no. We should, in fact, alert our handlers and turn her in.

Biscuit's eyes were locked on mine. I knew she was thinking the same thing. Zoe, however, had had such a pervasive undercurrent of sadness—all weekend long. Would it be right to turn her in and get her into trouble? I've heard humans say that some rules are made to be broken. Wouldn't it be better to allow Zoe this indulgence? To eat the french fry and not be a snitch? I nodded to Biscuit, and she put her teeth on the proffered item, delicately removing it from Zoe's fingers.

I held my breath and waited, hoping there would be another offering from above the table. Moments later, another french fry appeared. I did the right thing and took it from the little girl. Emily was my priority, but it didn't hurt me to be kind to others.

CHAPTER 15

Connor rolled his luggage over the threshold of his San Francisco condo. He slept during most of the long flight across the Pacific, but he was still exhausted. Sleeping on an airplane wasn't ever restful.

He dropped his keys on the small table to the left of the door, next to the notebook labeled "Welcome" that the vacation rental company supplied for people who had occupied the space almost every night since he'd been in Tokyo. His condo was in a desirable location, and the rental income had more than paid his mortgage. It had been a good business decision to rent his condo out while he was away, but he felt out of sync with the place now—as if he was just another temporary occupant and not like he was home.

Connor rubbed his hand across the stubble on his chin. If Emily were there, it would feel like home. He'd called and texted her during his layover, but she hadn't answered any of them. His efforts to win her back might be in vain, but he had to try.

He moved his suitcases to the bedroom and began a tour of the condo, inspecting the walls, furniture, and floors for signs of damage. The management company for the rental service had done a good job—the place was neat and tidy, and nothing he'd left behind was missing.

He walked to the front hall closet and unlocked it. He'd stashed all of their wedding presents there and installed a lock before he left. It held the cache of lovely items that their friends and family had selected for him and Emily to use in their new life together. The only things that weren't in the closet were the dishes, silverware, and glasses that he'd sent to Emily to use in her new apartment. It only seemed fair that she should have something from their marriage.

He opened the door and gave the contents a cursory inspection. Everything appeared to be in order. He stood in the doorframe, contemplating his next action.

He should take everything out of the closet and set it in its intended place. Maybe then, when Emily came home—if he could get her to come back to him—these gifts that had been meant to be shared by the two of them would convince her to stay.

He'd have time to attend to their wedding presents later. The most important thing he had to do was win Emily back.

Connor crossed to the desk in the alcove off the living room and sat down to compose a note to Emily. He'd been drafting it in his head since his first week in Tokyo. The new job had been everything he'd hoped it would be, and the city was fascinating, but he'd taken no pleasure in any of it. Emily was the center of his world, and his heart responded to her as if she was his true north.

He took a sheet of plain white paper from the desk and began writing, his pen pumping like a piston. The words poured out of him. Connor paused at the end of the second page and read what he'd written, his pen poised above the page. He cursed under his breath and crumpled the papers into a ball that he sent sailing toward the waste basket.

He began again. After another half dozen iterations, he laid the pen on the desk. He'd finally expressed what was in his heart.

Connor looked at his watch. It was after midnight, and he was now light-headed with fatigue. He'd crawl into bed for a few hours, then re-read what he'd written in the morning. If it still reflected his true feelings after he'd gotten some rest, he'd take it to Emily's apartment and leave it in her mailbox. He wouldn't let her go without putting up a fight.

Connor trudged into the bedroom and kicked off his shoes, sprawling onto the bed in the clothes he'd traveled in. He fell asleep thinking of Emily.

CHAPTER 16

*E*mily's hand hovered over the screen of her phone.

"Happy Birthday. Hope you had fun last night at the ballet, and you have a very special day today," read the voice of her phone.

Emily pressed send.

"Is that text to Gina—your friend we met at the makeup counter yesterday?"

"Yes."

"Is she your best friend?"

"She used to be."

"Why isn't she now?"

"It's … it's complicated, honey," Emily said.

"Why do adults always say that when they don't want to talk about something? I'm smart. I understand complicated things."

"I know you are." Emily sighed. "Sometimes people say that when they don't want to talk about things."

"Like maybe when you don't know how you feel about something?"

"Exactly."

Emily's phone pinged, signaling an incoming text.

"It's from Gina." Emily held her finger over the message.

"Thank you. I had such a good time last night. Craig is the nicest man I've ever dated. I'm so glad I ran into you yesterday. Thanks for remembering my birthday," read her phone.

Emily texted back: "I'm so glad! What was your dress like?"

Gina replied: "Sapphire satin that clung like a second skin. I starved myself all last week to make sure it would zip."

A second ping followed immediately: "I don't know if you can see it, but here's our photo."

Emily held the phone up to her left eye and moved it around, examining the image through the pinhole of her remaining vision. "Wow," she uttered.

"Can I see?" asked Zoe.

Emily handed her the phone.

"She looks so glamorous. And her boyfriend is super handsome."

"Isn't he? They look like models."

Emily typed back: "I can see this! He's a hottie, and you're gorgeous. Great dress. You look happy."

The reply was: "I am. Thank you for saying so. I miss you, Em."

Emily rested the phone against her chin.

"I think Gina wants to be friends again," Zoe said.

"I think you're right."

"It's nice to have friends."

"Yes—it is."

"So, are you going to be friends with Gina again?"

"I don't know, sweetie. I need to think about it." Emily laid her phone back on the kitchen table. "We've only got an hour until my mom arrives with dinner. I'd like to finish my braille homework, and you said you have to read two chapters in your book. Let's get back to work."

CHAPTER 17

$\mathcal{M}$artha found a parking spot on the street in the middle of the next block. She opened her trunk and began to gather the bags of groceries and additional kitchen items she knew Emily would find helpful, sliding the handles along her arm. Her eyes fell on the large box containing the deluxe chopper/blender. Emily had learned to use the model at Martha's, so she knew it would be a welcome addition to her daughter's kitchen.

Who was she kidding? She couldn't carry all this stuff at once. She'd purchased enough groceries for at least a fortnight. Knowing Emily was prepared gave her comfort. She'd take in the perishables now and enlist Zoe's help in collecting the rest.

Martha poked through the remaining bags in her trunk, rearranged her load on her arm, and set out toward Emily's building. She was concentrating on the stone steps leading to the front door when she heard a familiar voice calling her name.

"Martha," Connor said, rushing to her and grabbing one of the bags as its handles were about to tear.

"Connor! You're … what are you doing here?"

"Here, let me take these from you," he said, relieving her of her load.

"You're back?"

"Yes. I've taken a new position with my company—here at headquarters."

"Didn't you like Tokyo?"

"I would have—if Emily had been with me." He turned his face away. "I never should have gone—never should have left her. It was the biggest mistake of my life." His eyes swiveled to hers. "I came back to try to make things right with her."

"Did she see you?" Martha motioned to the building with her head. "Just now?"

"No. She hasn't answered any of my calls or texts. I got home yesterday and wrote her a note. I just left it in her mailbox."

"You moved back here without any encouragement from Emily?"

Connor shrugged. "I had to try. I couldn't just sit on my hands and wait."

Martha smiled thinly. "No. That wouldn't be like you at all."

"Has she mentioned me?"

Martha pursed her lips, then answered. "No."

He glanced at the building. "This place is old, but it looks well maintained. She's close to her work. How is she doing?"

"Her apartment is small but extremely comfortable. She's doing great. It's remarkable. She's excelled in everything at the foundation."

"That's not surprising. I've never known her not to excel."

"She's even learning to cook."

"Wow." Connor chuckled. "I never expected that."

Martha smiled at him.

"Would you—would you be willing to put in a good word for me? Convince Em to at least talk to me?" His voice was even, but his eyes were pleading.

"I agree that Emily needs to talk to you, Connor, but I'm not going to interfere. She's had so much to cope with since you got married. She'll know when she's ready."

He lowered his face to the ground, nodding. "Do you think she'll be ready soon?"

"I have no idea." Martha touched his arm. "I know that her blindness happened to both of you. And I'm so sorry—for you both. But this is something the two of you will have to work out. You'll have to be patient." She reached for the bags. "I'd better get these inside."

"I'll carry them for you," Connor said.

"I don't think that's a good idea."

"I won't try to weasel my way in to see her," Connor said. "I'll leave you at her doorstep."

"Thanks—I'd appreciate that." She led the way to the building and held the door for him. "I know you love my daughter, and I know you're trying."

"That means a lot to me, Martha. I wish I could rewrite the past, but I can't. All I can do now is focus on our future."

***

"You've got more?" Emily said, running her hands over the mound of shopping bags that Martha deposited on the kitchen counter.

"This is enough meat, dairy, and produce for a week or ten

days. I've got canned goods and spices in the car. Plus, a chopper/blender like mine and a balloon whisk."

"You've outdone yourself, Mom! This is so thoughtful of you."

"Zoe—can you help me carry in the rest?"

"Let me find my shoes."

"I've brought chicken thighs that I've been marinating in buttermilk. I got the recipe off the internet. It's supposed to be like Kentucky Fried Chicken—without all the fat. We'll use your air fryer—if that's ok?"

"Of course. I knew you'd be itching to give it a try."

"I can't deny that," Martha said as she approached the door.

"I'll get the rest of this sorted out," Emily said. "I'll use the app on my phone that scans barcodes to identify things for me. Zoe and I can label them while we make dinner."

The three generations of women set to work. By the time the chicken was cooked to crispy perfection, and the salad and rice Martha had prepared at home were on the table, Zoe and Emily had labeled and stashed everything Martha had brought.

"Verdict on the chicken?" Martha asked.

"As good as KFC," Emily said. "That was a wonderful meal, Mom."

"Gramma would like it," Zoe said. "She loves KFC."

"We'll have to make her some," Emily said. "When she comes home from the hospital."

"Could we?"

"You bet," Emily said. "I'll get the recipe from Mom, and I'll practice."

"Gosh—I never thought I'd share my love of cooking with you," Martha said. "This is fun." She stood and picked up her plate and Emily's. "I hate to eat and run, but Zoe has school tomorrow, so we'd better hit the road. We'll clean up and be on our way."

Emily stood. "You'll do no such thing. I'm perfectly capable of cleaning up my own kitchen."

"We don't mind …" Martha began.

"Nope. I've got this. It'll take you almost an hour to get home. Put whatever's in your hand to the right of the sink and grab your coat. Zoe—make sure you've got all your stuff."

"I put everything in my backpack before dinner."

"I'll walk you out," Emily said. "Garth needs a comfort break."

A chilly drizzle was beginning to fall when they stepped outside. The three hugged and said a quick goodbye.

Emily and Garth were heading to the patch of grass designated for use by the dogs in the building when Martha called to her.

"Check your mailbox, honey," she called.

"Why? There's no mail on Sunday."

"Just check your mailbox," came Martha's firm reply.

CHAPTER 18

*B*ecause Mom urged us to check our mailbox, I made quick work of doing my business. I could sense that Emily was curious, and so was I.

"Find mailbox," Emily said.

I took us to the wall of metal boxes at the back of the building on the ground floor.

Emily unlocked our mailbox and removed a single envelope.

"Someone must have dropped this off," she said, moving her hand across the envelope. "There's no stamp."

She brought the envelope to her nose. "I might be crazy, but it smells like Connor." She held the envelope out to me. "What do you think?"

I touched my nose to the paper and gave it a cursory sniff before quickly turning my head away. It was from Connor, all right. I'd memorized all the scents that were important to her. Connor was important, but in a bad way. He made Emily profoundly sad. I couldn't understand why he mattered so much to her.

"There's only one way to find out, right?" She sighed heavily before pulling up on my harness. "Find elevator," she said.

We started off.

"If it's from Connor. I don't think I want to read it," she said quietly. "I could always leave it for another day."

We walked in silence. I'd never counted patience as one of my Emily's long suits.

"I'm too curious to know what's in here," she said.

The elevator arrived. "Forward in," she said and located the button for our floor.

The elevator bounced to a stop and the doors opened with a clunk.

"Forward out," Emily commanded, followed by, "home."

I slowed my pace as I guided us home, trying to give her more time to think. I was painfully aware that she'd slept fitfully recently—tossing and turning all night long. Reading a letter from *him*—at bedtime—would not help her get a good night's sleep.

We entered the apartment, and Emily removed my harness. She placed it in its usual spot at the end of the sofa and put the envelope on the coffee table.

I made a beeline for my favorite spot on the carpet—the one that afforded me an unobstructed view of the kitchen. I circled three times and settled in, keeping my eyes on her the whole time.

"I have leftovers to put away and a kitchen to clean up," Emily said. "I need to do that first."

I thought that was an excellent idea. Maybe she'd even forget about the stupid letter.

"We'll open it before bedtime. I promise."

I sighed heavily. *I guess not.*

Emily packaged the leftover salad and chicken for tomorrow night's dinner and put her dishes in the dishwasher. After wiping down the countertops and kitchen table, she selected the dishwasher's normal cycle—the one I saw Zoe mark with a raised dot sticker—and pressed the start button.

She picked up her phone from the counter and made her way to the sofa.

I padded over to where she sat and put my head in her lap. She always massaged my ears when I did that. Except not this time.

She snatched the envelope from the coffee table.

Ignoring my ears, she gave her full attention to Connor's letter.

Emily moaned softly and sank back against the sofa cushions.

We'd had a busy, fun weekend. She'd connected with Gina again, and we were excited at the prospect of Stephanie and Biscuit living in our neighborhood. Did she want to spoil it all now? Whatever was in that envelope would disturb her hard-won equilibrium. I felt certain of that.

"I'm not alone, am I, boy? In anything. I'll always have you, won't I?"

Why was she even asking? Of course, she wasn't alone. She'd always have me. I was hers forever. I touched my nose to her chin and brushed it with a kiss.

She inhaled deeply and forced herself into an upright position. She stroked my back and planted a kiss on the top of my head. "Thank you for reminding me."

Emily inserted her thumb under the flap and opened the envelope, withdrawing a single sheet of paper. She spread it out flat on the coffee table and opened her text recognition app on her phone.

I leaned against her knee, staring at the paper and wishing, not for the first time, that I could read.

Emily moved the phone over the paper until the voice began reading. The envelope held a letter from Connor.

Every nerve in my body told me to be on high alert. I listened as that annoying voice in the tiny box said things that hurt Emily's heart and made her cry. I had half a mind to grab it out of her hand and toss it against the wall. I knew that would land me in big trouble.

Her breath caught in her throat as she listened.

My darling Em. I pray that I have the chance to say all of this to you, in person. I'm guessing that a voice-over program is reading this to you, and I'm sure that it won't convey the depth of emotion that I'm feeling.

I love you, Em. You're the one for me. Always have been—always will be. When we got married, we intended to forge a life together. I still want to do that. My time away from you has taught me that the only thing that has any true meaning is building a life with you. Like we'd planned and promised each other on our wedding day.

My thoughtless stupidity in cajoling you into that disastrous horseback ride resulted in you losing your eyesight. I take full respon-sibility for that. If you never forgive me, I understand. I can't forgive myself.

I have to know, Em. I can't go forward without seeing if you're willing to give us a shot. I've taken a position at our corporate head-quarters and have moved back into our condo. I've been to counseling to learn how to be a better partner, and I've researched how a sighted partner should accommodate their blind spouse. I should have done this before, and maybe it's too little too late ...

Please, Em, take your time and think about this. Think about us. I'm in no rush. We can take things as slowly as you'd like. I'm asking for the opportunity to be the husband you deserve; the husband I know I can be.

My unending love,

Connor

I waited patiently for the words to stop. Emily's tears told me she was upset, but the way she held her shoulders suggested that something else was going through her mind. Were these tears part happy and part sad?

I pushed my upper body onto the sofa and licked away her tears.

Emily laughed and rubbed my ears, kneading them in the way I loved best.

"Thank you, boy," she whispered, her chin resting on the top of my head. She reached over and slipped my harness over my head. "Are you tired? I'm exhausted. Let's go to bed early."

Later, after we'd both settled down to sleep, I heard her pat the bed next to her.

"Garth," she called softly.

She didn't have to ask me twice. I sprang onto the bed and curled up next to her.

Emily put an arm across my chest. I willed myself to stay awake until I felt her arm relax and heard her rhythmic breathing.

CHAPTER 19

*E*mily sat, head bent toward her computer, as she listened to her screen reader give voice to the symbols and characters in a line of computer code. She was concentrating so hard she missed the soft knocking on her office doorframe.

Dhruv cleared his throat.

Emily tapped the screen to pause the reader and turned toward him.

"Hi," she said. "Happy Monday."

"You're in early," Dhruv said.

"I woke up and started thinking about … a letter I received. I couldn't get back to sleep, so I finally got dressed and came in."

"I do that, sometimes, when I can't sleep. Did you get settled into your apartment?"

"Yes—thanks to you and my mom and Zoe. I appreciate everything you did for me."

"Good."

"I was wondering if your uncle might have another unit available soon?"

"Don't you like your apartment?"

"I'm not asking for myself. Zoe and I met up with a friend of mine from the foundation yesterday. She's planning to move into our neighborhood in the next month. I told her about my place and said I'd ask if there would be any openings in the building."

"There's nothing vacant right now," Dhruv said, "but I'll ask my uncle tonight. There might be something the first of the month."

"Terrific. Stephanie and Biscuit—she has a guide dog, too— are coming over this weekend to see my place."

"I like guide dogs," Dhruv said.

Emily couldn't suppress a smile. "You want to pet Garth, don't you?"

"Yes."

"Go ahead," Emily said. "You can greet him."

Dhruv dropped to one knee and ruffled Garth's ears.

"I should get back to work," Emily said, hoping that Dhruv would take the hint and let her resume her analysis of the problematic line of code.

"I still can't get over the speed setting of your voice-over program," Dhruv said.

"Think of how fast auctioneers talk," Emily continued. "You can still understand them."

"I've read that our brains fill in errors and gaps when we read written text, but we don't do that when we listen. Going through the code by listening to it might be better than seeing it on the screen."

"A lot of blind programmers would agree with that," Emily said. "I feel like I'm still getting used to working this way. One thing that's helpful is that I can adjust the speed on my screen reader. I can slow it way down and go character by character if I need to."

"I'll bet you're going to be really good at it."

"Thanks, Dhruv."

"What's that thing with the metal pins in it?"

"That looks like a keyboard? That's my braille reader. It's plugged into my computer and translates what's on the screen into braille."

"You can do both—listen and read."

"That's right."

"I've read about the grades of braille and the math version of braille called Nemeth. Don't they take years to learn?"

"They can. It turns out I have a real affinity for braille—sort of like how some people are good at learning different languages. I'm continuing to work with a teacher from the foundation on grade 2 and Nemeth. I have three hours of instruction—via the internet every week—and tons of homework."

"That's so neat." Dhruv rose and moved to the door. "You should tell them."

"Who should I tell—and what?" she asked.

"The others—that you're learning to do your job."

"I already know how to do my job, Dhruv." Emily narrowed her eyes. "What are people saying about me?"

Dhruv remained in the doorway, shifting his weight from foot to foot.

"Tell me."

"Nothing bad. They just don't know if you can do the same work you used to."

"Does that include you and the rest of the team?"

"Not me. I know you can do everything you used to do.

Michael thinks that it'll take time for you to be as fast as you used to be. Donna says we need to take it easy on you—give you time to adjust. I told them you're doing fine and are even faster than before."

"Thank you, Dhruv." She sucked in a deep breath and sank against the back of her chair. "I've noticed that the team isn't bringing me as many problems as they used to. I thought our workload might have slowed down."

"It hasn't."

"This is so frustrating." Emily threw her hands in the air. "Have you noticed me making mistakes? Be honest with me, Dhruv."

"No. You haven't."

"Have you told the rest of the team?"

"Yes," he said, "but they don't listen to me. They think I'm too loyal."

Emily suppressed a smile. Dhruv was, indeed, unshakably loyal. "What can I do to convince them?"

"Tell the team what you just told me. Bring them in here to work with you so they can see for themselves."

"That's a good idea," Emily said. She spun back to her computer screen and began to type. "I'm going to hold office hours this afternoon. I'm sending an email to the team. Everyone needs to sign up for a thirty-minute segment and bring me something they're having trouble with. We're going to work on it together."

"I know just what I want to bring in," Dhruv replied.

"Terrific. I can't wait to look at it. I'm going to show them that I may have lost my sight, but I didn't lose my brain or my ability to do this job."

CHAPTER 20

*E*mily was having lunch at her desk—again. I liked it much better when we stretched our legs and went somewhere. Even if it was foggy or rainy, I loved a midday break. I found it cleared the cobwebs from my brain and made me more alert in the afternoon.

The salad we'd picked up from the lunch cart in the lobby sat in its unopened Styrofoam container at the edge of her desk. She leaned toward her computer, and the voice in the machine droned on endlessly while Emily tapped at her keyboard. She was always a fast typist but today was pounding away at warp speed. I suspected her reaction might have something to do with Dhruv's earlier visit. I was turning this puzzling development over in my mind when the clacking of keys stopped suddenly, and Emily attacked her salad with the same vigor.

At least she was eating. Whatever was going on with her, I knew she needed a good lunch to keep her energy up.

She'd just thrown the empty Styrofoam container in the trash when the man called Michael stepped into her office. I liked Michael. His voice was always full of caring—just like it was now.

"I think I'll have this figured out by the morning," he said, sitting in the chair on the other side of her desk. "No need for you to ..."

"I looked at what you're working on." Emily cut him off. "I can see the problem."

"Oh ..."

I heard him suck in a big breath.

"Really?"

"Yes. Let me show you." Emily turned her computer screen toward him. She activated the voice reader and held up one hand, listening. "There!" she exclaimed as she stopped the reader. "Did you hear that?"

"Frankly, no," Michael said. "He was talking too fast. I couldn't understand anything he said."

Emily leaned toward him, resting on her forearms, and crossed her ankles under the desk. One of the ankles bounced against the other. Unless I was mistaken, Emily was feeling quite pleased with herself.

"I'm sorry," Emily said in a tone of voice that told me she wasn't. "It takes a while to learn to listen at that speed."

"Do you ... do you listen to your emails that fast?"

Emily shook her head. "Faster."

"Holy cow," Michael said. "I can't even read that fast."

"The screen should be paused at the point in the code that contains the error. Can you see it?"

Michael's shoes shuffled closer to the center of the desk as he bent toward the screen. "Yes! Oh my gosh—there it is. I've been looking at this string of code for two days and didn't see it."

"I've found that listening can be a powerful tool," Emily said.

"I'll say it is."

"Do you have what you need to close out this request?"

"I do. Thanks for doing this, Em. Calling us all in."

"You're welcome. My job is to help you."

"I know. We all know that. We didn't want to overwhelm you. We thought we were giving you a chance to settle in."

A middle-aged woman walked to the doorway. "Want me to come back? I think I'll have my issue resolved by the end of the day. I don't need …"

Michael and Emily both laughed.

"We're done. In ten minutes, Emily found the problem that I've been looking for all week." He stood. "Get in here. She's baaack!"

Michael left the room, and Donna took the spot across from Emily.

"Would you like me to open the project I've been working on?"

"I pulled it up earlier while I was eating lunch." Emily ran her mouse over the screen until the screen reader read the name of the tab she wanted to open.

"There's a glitch in the code," Donna said. "I think I know where it has to be."

"Let's listen for it," Emily said, holding up a hand to silence Donna.

They both remained silent as the screen reader read the code to them.

"There!" both women said in unison.

"That's got to be where the problem is," Donna said. "It's not even close to where I thought it was."

"I agree—that's the segment of code you need to fix."

"Thanks, Em. You've saved me a ton of time."

"I'm glad I could help." Emily was smiling. "I'm impressed

that you could keep up with the screen reader. Dhruv and Michael say it's too fast."

"I listen to audiobooks and podcasts during my commute," Donna said. "Over the years, I've increased the speed. I guess that helped."

"It's a learned skill, without a doubt."

I turned on my side and tucked my nose under my tail. It was time to recharge my batteries while my Emily did her thing.

I awakened to a pair of familiar hands rubbing my ears. Ahhh ... Dhruv. When had he come in? Sometimes that man was as quiet as a ghost—or else I had fallen into deep doggie REM sleep. No matter—I was awake now. I wagged my tail in appreciation of his ministrations.

CHAPTER 21

"Will Gramma know me?" Zoe asked as she and Martha headed down the long hallway to Irene's room. Overhead fluorescent lights reflected in the shiny surface of the immaculate linoleum floors.

"Of course she will. Why do you ask?"

"She sounded so ... odd ... on the phone."

"That was on the day after surgery, and she was on strong pain medication. She'll be better today." Martha looked down at Zoe. "Did that scare you, honey?"

Zoe shrugged.

"People always feel the worst right after surgery." Martha drew to a stop and checked the room number on the door. The faint bleep of monitors came from every direction. "Here we are." She could see a pair of feet under a blanket in the hospital bed inside the room. Martha tapped lightly on the partially open door. "It's Martha and Zoe," she called.

"Come in," came a hoarse reply.

Martha put her arm around Zoe's shoulders, and they

entered together.

Irene was lying in bed with the head raised to a sitting position. She held out her arms to her granddaughter. "Zoe," she said before dissolving into a coughing fit.

Zoe walked slowly to the bedside.

"Are you okay? Your voice sounds funny."

Martha handed Irene a cup of water with a straw from the bedside table.

Irene held the cup to her mouth, chased the straw with her lips, and took a sip. "My throat's a little sore from the anesthesia tube," she said. "Perfectly normal—happens all the time."

She reached a hand toward Zoe, who grasped it with both of hers.

"How're you doing?" Martha asked.

"Good—or so they tell me. The surgery went fine. They got me up and walking yesterday, and that was tough, let me tell you."

"Did you walk today?" Zoe asked.

"Yes. I just finished and got back in bed before you arrived." She pointed to a walker pushed against the wall. "I'll be using that thing to help me get around for a while. It makes me feel ancient, but I'll need to use it." She squeezed Zoe's hand. "I hope you won't be ashamed of your old grandmother, with that thing."

"No way," Zoe said. "Lots of grandmas have them."

"Have they said when you'll be coming home?" Martha asked.

"I was hoping by the end of the week," Irene replied. "The physical therapist said that I might need to go to a rehabilitation hospital for several weeks until I'm good and steady on my feet."

Zoe's chin jerked up.

"I told him I couldn't be away from my granddaughter that long—that we'd have to do whatever was necessary so I could go home by this weekend."

Zoe smiled.

"If you have to go somewhere else for a while, Zoe can continue to stay with me. We're having a great time, aren't we, Zoe?"

"I'm fine with Martha," Zoe said. "Sabrina is, too. And I got to spend the weekend with Emily. At her new apartment."

"That was nice," Irene said. She looked past Zoe to Martha and raised her eyebrows.

"Zoe helped Emily organize her place and label everything with braille tags and dots. She said Zoe was a huge help."

"I met a new friend of Emily's, too. Stephanie also has a guide dog."

"Sounds like you're having a good time." She cupped Zoe's chin in her hand. "I'm so proud of what a kind and helpful girl you are." Irene's eyes grew moist. "You're just like your mother was at your age."

Zoe clung to her grandmother's hand as she looked around the room, taking in the monitors, pull cords, and equipment. "There's a lot of stuff in here."

"All hospital rooms have these things," Irene said, "whether the patient needs them or not. It's nothing to worry about."

"Is there anything you need? Can I bring you something from home?" Martha asked.

"How about a clean pair of sweats and a T-shirt to wear when I get out of here? You'll find them in the top drawer of my dresser."

"Any preferences?"

"Whatever's on top will be fine. I'm not going to be fussy."

"I think I know your wardrobe well enough to find your favorites. I'll bring them the next time we visit."

"I don't want the two of you running back and forth to see me. We can talk on the phone every day, and I'll be home in no time." She studied Zoe. "I don't think hospitals are easy places for children." Irene yawned involuntarily.

"You must be exhausted," Martha said. "No one ever gets a good night's sleep in a hospital."

"That walk tired me out," Irene replied, lifting one hand and smoothing Zoe's hair.

"Let's get out of here so you can rest. Are you ready, Zoe?"

The little girl nodded.

Irene drew Zoe toward her and kissed her cheek. "Be a good girl. I know you always are. I'll be back home before you know it."

Zoe's eyes were solemn. "You promise?"

"I promise," Irene said. "And give Sabrina a big hug from me. I love you, honey. Don't worry about a thing."

***

"Hi, Zoe." The tone of Zoe's voice had triggered alarm bells in Emily. Something was bothering her young friend. "What's up?"

"You said we could talk every day since we don't see each other on Martha's porch like we used to."

"Of course we can. How was school today?"

"Fine. School's always fine."

"That's good." She silently waited for Zoe to continue.

"It's Gramma," Zoe finally said in a small voice.

"Mom texted me that you went to see her. She said that they're walking her around, and she's doing great."

"That's what they told me."

"Then what's wrong?"

"I dunno. It's just a feeling I have."

"Oh, sweetie. Don't imagine things."

"You think she's okay?"

"If the doctors say she is, then I do."

"She may not be able to come home right away."

"That's relatively common. Nothing to worry about. You and Sabrina can stay with my mom. You're happy there, aren't you?"

"Yes. Sabrina especially. She likes your yard."

Emily laughed. "We seem to have more rabbits than you do, don't we?"

"Yeah. Sabrina loves to chase rabbits. Even if she can't catch them."

"I'll bet that's fun to watch."

Emily heard her mother's voice in the background.

"I have to take my bath and get ready for bed."

"Okay, honey. Try not to worry, but you can call me any time—day or night—if you need to talk."

"Thanks, Emily."

Emily heard a firm knock on her door. "My dinner delivery is here. I've got to go. Sweet dreams, sweet girl. All will be well. You'll see."

CHAPTER 22

I don't like to complain, but dinner was late tonight.

When I was at the Guide Dog Center, one of my favorite things was their strict observance of mealtimes. It was a civilized practice that I approved of.

Emily set a bag on the kitchen counter. I lifted my nose in the air. This wasn't her usual turkey curry. She was trying something new.

I sidled over to her.

"I'll bet you're hungry, too, aren't you, boy? We've had a long day." She scooped kibble into my bowl and set it in front of me. "Here you go."

I wagged my tail and tucked into my dinner. Emily always thought of others first.

I had just begun to eat when she cursed and pushed the bag with her takeout away from her. She raced to the door.

I reluctantly stopped eating and moved toward her. If we had somewhere to go, that was part of my job description.

Emily grasped her cane and her keys and hurtled through the door, slamming it behind her before I caught up to her.

What was this? Was she going somewhere without me?

I stared at the door, perplexed. Her coat remained on the hook.

It was a chilly night. Surely she wasn't going outside without her coat. Or me.

I retraced my steps to my bowl and finished my dinner without my usual relish. I got a drink of water and settled on my after-dinner spot by the sofa. She'd be back soon.

I tried to get comfortable, but as the clock on the wall ticked away the minutes, my anxiety grew. Where was my Emily?

CHAPTER 23

*E*mily made her way as quickly as possible to the elevator. If she were lucky, she'd intercept the delivery man in the lobby. Since he'd mixed up her order with someone else's, her dinner was probably sitting in a bag on his backseat. If she could just catch up with him, they could exchange bags, and everyone would be happy.

The elevator was waiting and took her to the ground floor without stopping.

Emily stepped out and called, "Sir," hoping the delivery man was in the lobby. She received no response.

Swinging her cane in front of her, Emily made her way out of the building and onto the sidewalk. The air smelled moist with fog. Maybe he was getting into his car. "Sir. Sir!" she called again.

Emily stopped and listened. Other than a car traveling down the other side of the street, there were no traffic sounds. The delivery man had already left.

"Damn it," Emily said under her breath. "I want my turkey

curry." She pulled out her phone and called the restaurant. She ordered food from them at least twice a week. The hostess who answered recognized her voice. Emily explained her problem.

"I'm so sorry. We'll send out a new order as soon as possible."

"How long will that take?"

"Our deliveries are running about an hour."

"That long?"

"It's the peak of the dinner rush," she said apologetically. "If you can come pick it up, I can have it for you in fifteen minutes."

Emily pulled her sweater close around herself. She was hungry and wanted her food now. She could walk to the restaurant and pick up her food. She knew it was close to her apartment. "Let's do that."

"Great. See you soon." The hostess hung up.

Emily opened the wayfinding app on her phone and spoke the name of the restaurant into it. The app quickly responded that it was three-tenths of a mile away.

Emily brought her phone to her lips, thinking. Wasn't Spencer, her mobility instructor at the foundation, constantly reminding her to keep practicing her cane skills? He had told her to go out without Garth, so she kept those skills sharp. Wouldn't now be an appropriate time to act on that advice? Walking to the restaurant wouldn't take more than ten minutes. She'd be back in no time—with her food. Her sweater was warm enough for such a short outing.

Emily's stomach growled. She pushed the 'go' button on her app and began walking, swinging her cane in front of her. The voice on her phone directed her.

The fog that had burned off during the day was now a heavy presence. The moisture clung to Emily's skin and pooled at the back of her neck. Despite the growing chill, she began to sweat from exertion.

A dog barked in the distance.

Emily continued on the path directed by the app. The sounds of the busy street in front of her became muffled by the fog. She tightened her grip on her phone, wishing she'd accepted her mobility instructor's offer to help her become more familiar with her neighborhood.

It was less than a third of a mile. She could do this. She continued walking another ten feet before her cane became ensnared by a metal post on her right. She stumbled and dropped her cane, catching herself before she fell.

Emily inhaled and exhaled rhythmically to steady herself. She stooped and picked up her cane from where it lay at her feet. Using her cane, she carefully explored the hazard that had tripped her up. She took a step toward the object and reached out a hand to confirm her suspicion. She grasped a metal handle that ran parallel to the sidewalk and pulled. A door creaked open on noisy hinges, and she placed her other hand into an open slot.

Emily smiled. She'd found the neighborhood mailbox. It would make an ideal landmark when she was out and about. She put the tip of her cane on the sidewalk and continued her journey. The app directed her to make one left turn and then a right. It told her the restaurant was one hundred fifty feet ahead, on her left.

The fog was heavy, shrouding every streetlight. The absolute blackness was unnerving. She remembered the rope lights that Dhruv had installed in her apartment and appreciated them more than ever. She made a mental note to thank him, again, the next time she saw him.

Her cane suddenly jumped from the sidewalk on its next

sweep to her left. She stopped and ran her cane over the obstruction in her path. Had she veered to the right or left without knowing it?

She found the edges of the sidewalk on either side of her. She was where she was supposed to be, in the middle of the sidewalk. Emily shuffled toward the obstruction until she felt cone-shaped objects to her right and left, with tape stretched between them. She inched her cane under the tape and felt the jagged edge of the concrete sidewalk give way to rubble.

Construction work. She dropped to her knees and placed her face close to the ground, trying to see through the pinhole of vision in her left eye. The fog entrapped any shard of light, making it impossible for her to see anything.

She got back to her feet and carefully skirted around the barrier with her cane, extending it to her left and feeling the even surface of the sidewalk. She continued walking, counting her steps under her breath.

"Two hundred," she muttered and pulled up short. She should have reached her destination by now. She bit her lip. Why hadn't her phone given her directions?

Emily tapped at the screen of her phone. It remained silent. She tapped again.

Was the battery dead? Her hand began to shake. That was ridiculous. She never let it get below a forty percent charge. She wiped the screen along her sweater and tried again, using the techniques she'd learned at the foundation. It still didn't respond.

"Damn it!"

She pressed the combination of buttons that would allow her to reboot her phone. Still nothing.

Emily took another five steps forward, then stopped and listened. A restaurant would be noisy at this time of day with the sounds of doors opening and closing and snippets of conversation spilling onto the sidewalk. The night was silent.

Emily's heart hammered in her chest. Acid pooled in the back of her throat, and she feared she might be sick. She was lost—truly lost. She was living the nightmare that stalked every blind person.

She stood on the sidewalk, jabbing at her unresponsive phone with increasing force. Tears began rolling down her cheeks.

CHAPTER 24

I may not be able to tell time, but I'm acutely aware of the passage
of time. Emily had been gone—without her coat or me
—for way
too long. We'd never been separated like this in all the time
we'd been together.

I got to my feet and stationed myself by the door, straining
to catch any sound from the hallway. I'd recognize Emily's foot-
falls as she approached. The elevator chimed, and I leaned
closer to the door. Someone got off, turned and walked in the
opposite direction.

I began to pant and padded over to my water bowl, more for
something to do than out of genuine thirst. My mind raced as I
lapped at the water. What was I going to do?

I resumed my post at the door. My anxiety grew with each
tick of the clock. Something was very wrong. I knew it in the
sixth sense that all dogs possess.

I barked a couple of times. I knew this was verboten, but I

couldn't help myself. I ran my nose along the bottom of the door, snuffling to catch any hint of Emily's approaching scent.

I sank back onto my rear haunches and pawed the door, and that's when it happened. My right front paw caught the latch of the inside door handle. I pushed down, and the door opened a crack.

I brought my front feet back to the ground and shoved my nose into the crack, pushing the door open. I was down the hall, to the elevator, in a flash. I knew the drill by heart.

The elevator was waiting for me. I stepped inside and pushed the button for the ground floor, just like I'd done with Emily every day.

I was moving, now. Doing something. It felt good to be taking action.

The elevator bumped to a stop on the ground floor, and I raced toward the front door. I needed to get out of here and go look for my Emily.

I pressed against the heavy glass, but it wouldn't budge. A metal bar halfway up appeared to be keeping it in place. I stared at it, trying to figure out how to get free. I began to do something I *never* did—not when I first met that she-devil-cat Liloh or when the phony service dog attacked me in the restaurant—I began to whine.

I was so wrapped up in my misery, I didn't hear the man approaching from behind. A pair of kind hands placed themselves around my chest.

Dhruv dropped to one knee. "Hey, buddy. What're you doing out here? Where's Emily?"

I turned my muzzle to him and looked into his eyes.

Dhruv understood. "Something's wrong, isn't it, Garth? You don't have your harness on. You got out, and now you can't find your way home, can you?"

What was he talking about? Me—not find my way home? Preposterous. He didn't understand. I barked and pawed at the door.

"Come on," he said, grabbing my collar. "Let's take you back upstairs."

I initially resisted but quickly realized that he needed to see for himself that Emily wasn't there. I followed him into the elevator and then sprinted down the hall to our apartment.

Dhruv stepped through our open door, calling, "Emily." With each unanswered call, his voice grew louder. He walked to the kitchen counter and picked up the unopened takeout bag. Dhruv turned back to me. "Something's wrong with Emily, isn't it?"

Bingo! Now he understood.

He snatched my leash from its hook by the door and affixed it to my collar. "Let's go, boy. We're going to find her." His voice caught on the last words.

My ears came up, and my muscles tensed. I wasn't in my working harness, but I was devoting everything I had to this task. We needed to find my Emily.

CHAPTER 25

*E*mily used the hem of her sleeve to wipe the tears from her

face. The fog had permeated her sweater, making it damp and clammy. She shivered. She was lost, and she had to find her way home. What had Spencer always told her? Take deep breaths until she calmed down and then think. He'd taught her strategies to employ in such a situation.

She inhaled to the count of six and exhaled to the count of six. Calling someone who knew where you were going was one thing they recommended. She hadn't told anyone—and her phone wasn't working. Her pulse began to race again. She took another deep breath.

Asking for help was also good. Emily cleared her throat and projected her voice into the darkness. "I'm blind, and I need help."

She waited in silence for the reply that never came. Tears began

to course down her cheeks again.

She heard a car door slam somewhere in front of her. She shuffled toward it, yelling, "Wait. Wait! HELP!"

The engine turned over.

"NO!" Emily bellowed. She filled her lungs and screamed, "STOP!"

The car shifted into gear and pulled away, the sound receding into the distance. She bent over, placed her hands on her knees, and sobbed out her fear and frustration.

Something rustled in the grass to her right. Emily stifled a scream and stood bolt upright. She struck out with her cane, hitting a small, soft object with a thump.

A cat screeched and ran off in the other direction.

Emily forced herself to concentrate on her breathing, batting her tears aside. Standing on a sidewalk crying and feeling sorry for herself wasn't getting her anywhere. She was in her own neighborhood in the early evening. She was going to be fine.

She put her cane on the sidewalk and turned herself around one hundred eighty degrees. She'd count to two hundred ten steps. If she hadn't reached the sidewalk construction that she'd encountered before, she'd turn around and come right back to this spot. She'd then turn ninety degrees and do the same thing. Even if she'd gotten herself totally turned around, she'd only have to do this three times before she was bound to find the construction.

From there, she'd retrace her steps to the mailbox. The two

turns her phone app had directed her to take were at the first intersections she'd encountered, and she remembered which way

she'd been told to turn. All she had to do was reverse directions.

Even if it took her until midnight, she could do this. She was close to home. Nothing was going to happen to her.

She sucked in a ragged breath. Garth must be anxious without her. She never left him home alone.

Emily straightened. The fog felt like a heavy blanket being held over her head. She pushed her shoulders back. Standing still wasn't moving her closer to home. She extended her cane to her right and stepped out to meet it.

CHAPTER 26

I swung my nose across the sidewalk and instantly found the scent I loved best in the world: Emily. She'd turned left when she'd come out of our building.

I glanced back at Dhruv and pulled in the direction of the scent.

"You've got her, haven't you, boy? Lead the way."

I stepped out in my fastest walking gate. Dhruv jogged to keep up with me.

The fog enveloped us, restricting visibility to a few feet. My nose was still good at a long distance.

We'd moved almost to the end of the first block when a fresh wave of scent washed over me. I leaped in the air and barked, then took off running.

Dhruv lost his grip on my leash.

I kept going, dragging it behind me. A tall, rectangular blue object was emerging from the fog. Approaching that object from the opposite direction was the person I loved best.

"Garth?" Emily cried.

I barreled up to her, putting on the brakes just before I collided with her. My tail was wagging so hard that I lost my balance and fell onto the sidewalk.

Emily dropped to her knees and flung her arms around my neck.

I tried to still myself, but couldn't manage it. I had to wiggle and squirm.

Emily kissed the top of my head. "You were worried about me, weren't you, boy?"

"We both were," Dhruv said, catching up with us.

"Dhruv?"

"Yes."

"How on earth did you … and Garth … get out here?"

Emily continued to massage my neck while Dhruv answered her questions.

Emily stood and took my leash. Her voice was thick with emotion as she told Dhruv what had transpired. "Garth knew, didn't he? He knew I'd gotten lost?"

"He sensed something was wrong."

"I never should have gone out without him. It was so stupid of me."

Dhruv considered this. "I don't think that's logical. Your phone froze. That's not your fault. There was construction that got in

your way. Again, not your fault. You were almost to the mailbox when we found you."

"That's true."

"You would have found your way home from there."

"That was my plan."

"You see—you got lost and got yourself out of it."

"I guess so. But this has been … terrifying." Emily shivered.

"Come on," Dhruv said. "You must be freezing." He removed

his jacket and placed it around her shoulders. "Let's go home." He placed Emily's hand on his elbow and began to lead them.

"Where were you going when you encountered Garth on the loose?"

"I was headed to a restaurant to pick up my dinner. I'd gotten delivery from that Thai place around the corner. They mixed up my order. Brought me turkey curry, which I hate."

Emily threw back her head and laughed. "You're not going to believe this. I think I know who has your dinner."

I trotted along next to them. I could sense that things were getting back to normal. For my part, I was exhausted. I wanted to go to bed. I hoped that Emily would make another exception to the 'no dogs on the bed' rule. I needed a good snuggle.

CHAPTER 27

*C*onnor shifted the enormous bunch of lilacs to the crook of his left arm. He raised his right hand to knock but stopped short. He'd told Emily that he'd give her time—he'd wait for her to contact him. He bent and propped the bouquet against the door.

The elevator doors opened at the end of the hallway.

Connor sucked in a breath as Emily and Garth got off the elevator and approached him. He backed soundlessly away from her doorway. His pulse quickened, and he wondered if his heart would explode in his chest. There she was—Emily— coming towards him. In another three steps, she'd be close enough for him to sweep her into his arms.

Garth took her to the door of her apartment. Emily felt for the lock and inserted her key. The door swung open, and the flowers fell inside.

"What's this?" Emily bent and grasped the flowers, bringing them to her nose. "Lilacs." She inhaled deeply. "Who in the world left me flowers?" She held them out to Garth. "What do you think, boy? Aren't they the best?"

Garth touched the blooms with his nose and sneezed loudly. He turned his head in Connor's direction and continued to sneeze.

Connor took a step back.

Emily's head snapped up. "Who's there?" Her voice was full of alarm.

Connor froze in place.

"Connor? Is that you?"

He cleared his throat. "Yes, Em. It's me."

She turned toward the sound of his voice, and they stood in silence.

"How did you know?"

"Who else would bring me lilacs—on the anniversary of our first date."

"You remembered."

"Of course I remember."

"I brought you lilacs, then, and you said they were your favorite." He swallowed hard. "I've always thought they helped me clinch that second date."

"They might have." She paused, then asked, "Why are you here?"

"I wanted to do something nice for you."

"I thought you were going to give me time. You said you'd wait for me to contact you."

"Then you read my note?"

"I did."

"Good." His breathing was labored as he waited for her to continue.

Emily remained silent.

"The truth is, I brought those flowers hoping they would

convince you to contact me. I know I said I'd give you time, but I'm not very patient. It's one of the things I need to work on."

"Patience is not your long suit—it's not in your DNA to wait for anything you want."

"I'm sorry, Em. I'm trying." He took a step closer. "You look great. The way you and Garth came down that hall—you're so sure of yourself. I'm impressed."

"Thank you. I've come a long way, but I still have a lot to learn." She reached down and stroked the top of Garth's head. "This guy is the best help imaginable."

"I can see that." Connor sighed. "Are you just getting home from work?"

"Yep."

"Would you like to get something to eat?"

"No." She shook her head.

"Ah … okay," he said, his voice thick with sadness.

"I can't tonight. I've got a test tomorrow that I need to study for. I'm learning Nemeth braille."

"That's impressive."

"You know what it is?"

"I've been getting up to speed about … about your new world."

"Thank you for doing that," Emily said quietly. "I've been working hard."

"What about dinner the day after tomorrow? After your test?"

Emily brought the flowers back to her nose and inhaled deeply. "How about coffee—on Sunday afternoon?"

"That'd be great, too," Connor replied in a rush. "I'll come by at two to pick you up?"

"I'll meet you at two at the coffee shop around the corner."

"Perfect. I can't wait."

Emily could hear that he was rocking from foot to foot.

"Good luck on your test tomorrow. You'll nail it."

"Thank you, Connor," Emily said, stepping across her threshold, with Garth at her heels. "And thank you for the flowers. They're lovely."

Connor stayed until he heard her deadbolt click into place. He turned and made his way to the elevator with a spring in his step that hadn't been there for months.

CHAPTER 28

*B*iscuit sneezed loudly as soon as she stepped into our apartment. Maybe she was allergic to those stupid flowers Connor had brought to Emily, too. I crossed to the coffee table, pointed my nose at the flowers, and cut my eyes to Emily. I was hoping she'd notice and put two and two together. I'd been sneezing all week. It was time for those flowers to go to the dumpster. Emily and Stephanie, however, were busy chatting up a storm.

"You've got everything all set up for yourself." Stephanie ran her hand along the counter. "I'm impressed."

"Thanks. My mom and Zoe helped me label stuff. I love living here, and I'm doing everything I always could. I'm feeling … normal again." Emily replied.

"That's why I want to live on my own." Stephanie explored the smart oven with her fingers. "How're you doing with cooking? I remember that you said you never learned to cook when you were sighted."

"Everyone thought I was kidding, but I wasn't. I didn't even know how to scramble an egg. Now that I've learned some of the basics, I'm enjoying it."

"This is a smart oven, isn't it? I think you've got every appliance and tool that the foundation recommended."

"I do. I'll bet you'd love this stuff. Why don't you come over after you've moved to the city and try things out before you decide if you want to buy anything? I remember that you're an excellent cook."

"That's a great idea."

"We can cook together, and you can teach me how to make some of your favorite recipes if you wouldn't mind. I've got this dream of having my mom over for a fancy dinner—that I've cooked."

"Sounds like fun. I'd love to help you if I can."

I led Biscuit to my favorite spot on the carpet, where the morning sunshine created lovely warm patches to doze in. Biscuit was a fast learner—she curled up next to me, and we both settled down to catch a few winks.

"You know what this feels like?" Emily asked. She continued without waiting for a response. "It feels like a couple of girlfriends making plans."

"We are girlfriends," Stephanie replied. "But I know what you mean. It all feels so normal."

"I'm glad you'll be living close by," Emily said.

"I used to walk down this street on my way to school," Stephanie said. "With my older brother and my cousin. It all feels remarkably familiar. I already know my way to the school where I'll be teaching. Did you ask about any vacancies in this building?"

"Dhruv didn't know of any, but he was going to ask his uncle. I'll follow up with him at work on Monday."

"Awesome. Fingers crossed that there will be."

"I'd better get going. My brother is picking me up out front in fifteen minutes to give me a ride back to our mom's. I'd like to give Biscuit a comfort break before we get in the car."

Emily roused me and put my harness around my neck. "We'll go to the area in back of the building where I take him."

The four of us made our way to the ground floor.

"Emily?" came the familiar voice as we were leading Stephanie and Biscuit out the back door.

I raised an eyebrow at Dhruv, and he nodded to me. After our outing to find Emily, we now shared a special bond.

"Dhruv. Hi!" Emily said.

"Hi," he replied. "Who's this?"

"This," Emily said, stepping to one side, "is my friend Stephanie Wolf. She and I were in the same class at the foundation. And this is her guide, Biscuit."

"Nice to meet you, Stephanie and Biscuit."

"I work with Dhruv," Emily explained.

"Emily told us all about you at the foundation," Stephanie said.

"Yeah," Dhruv muttered.

"She told us how helpful you were in convincing her to enroll in their program. Not many people are lucky enough to have a friend as dedicated and knowledgeable as you."

Neither woman could see the flush rising above his collar.

"Dhruv has been a lifesaver for me from the very beginning," Emily said. "Even recently, but that's a story for another time."

"I ... I'd better go," he stammered before turning abruptly to the door.

"Wait," Emily said. "Did you ask your uncle about any openings in this building?"

"He said no—there aren't."

Stephanie let out a heavy sigh. "I'm sure I'll find somewhere else." She stuck out her right hand in his direction.

Dhruv stared at it, then took it in his right, and they shook hands.

"Nice to meet you, Dhruv. Any friend of Emily's is a friend of mine."

Dhruv straightened, and his shoulders relaxed. He continued to clasp her hand. "Thank you, Stephanie. I like that."

"You're welcome," she said. "I hope I see you again. I'll be back—I'm going to teach Emily how to cook."

"Maybe you can come to dinner, Dhruv. You can be our guinea pig," Emily said.

"I can do that. I like to eat, and I'm not fussy."

Stephanie laughed. "Sounds like the perfect man to cook for."

Dhruv dropped Stephanie's hand. "See you," he said before he continued on his way.

"Dhruv's a bit socially awkward," Emily said. "He's ..."

"He's charming," Stephanie interrupted. "Shy and unassuming. From what you've told me, he's thoughtful and notices other

people's needs."

"He certainly does. He's also one of the most brilliant people I've ever met—and definitely the kindest."

"Lucky you," Stephanie said.

I took a step toward the back door. I could tell by the way my friend's tail twitched that she needed to reach our destination. "Dhruv's been a very good friend to me, in addition to being the most talented programmer on my team."

"So that's ... that's all he is to you?"

"Of course. I'm married, remember? You like him, don't you?" Emily asked.

"I ... I do. Do you think I'm crazy?"

"Not at all." Emily's voice reflected the smile that washed over her face. "Dhruv would make the most wonderful boyfriend."

"Is he dating anyone?"

"Nope." Emily clasped her hands together. "You know what we do now?"

"No. What?"

"What girlfriends have been doing for each other for ages. I'll talk to him—see if he likes you."

"Don't be too obvious," Stephanie said. "I don't want to look foolish."

"No worries," Emily said. "I've got this. We always chat about our weekends on Monday mornings. I'll find out then."

"Thank you. You'll let me know, won't you? Either way?"

"Sure. But don't worry, Stephanie. I don't know why, but I think he likes you."

"I'd better go. My brother texted while we were chatting with Dhruv. He's waiting out front."

"Have a good rest of the weekend. I'll call as soon as I've talked to Dhruv." Emily chuckled. "This is so fun!"

Biscuit and I bumped noses before she led Stephanie to the front door. I stretched out my front paws, then took us back to our apartment with extra spring in my step. If Emily and Stephanie were going to spend more time together, that meant that I'd be seeing more of Biscuit. Things were going swell.

CHAPTER 29

*C*onnor pushed his chair back and stood, raising his hand to wave at the beautiful, auburn-haired woman silhouetted in the doorway of the coffee shop. He caught himself and brought it back to his side. He moved toward her, calling her name.

Emily turned to him.

"I'm here," he said. "Can I guide you?"

"Just lead the way. Garth and I will follow."

Connor traced a serpentine path through the maze of small round tables with metal chairs drawn up to them at haphazard angles.

"Thanks for meeting me here," Connor said as they took their seats at the table he'd secured for them.

"We got here early," Emily said. "I'm surprised we didn't beat you here."

"I wanted to get a table. It was busy when I arrived—I had to wait ten minutes. The crowd's thinned out now."

"Connor Harrington, III—early? That's a first."

"You see? I can change." His voice was playful. "I also wanted to be here when you arrived—in case you needed ..."

"Help?"

"Yes ... I suppose so."

"I go places all the time, Connor."

"I didn't want you to have to wait alone."

Emily stroked Garth's side. "I'm never alone."

"I can see that." He cleared his throat. "Can I get you a caramel macchiato—with an extra shot, no whip? Is that still your drink of choice?"

Emily laughed. "I'd love one. It smells so good in here—I'm practically salivating. Thank you."

Connor stepped to the counter, eventually returning with her drink and a cup for himself.

"Still a black coffee guy?"

"How can you tell?"

"The smell's a dead giveaway."

"Ah ... seems like you're doing amazingly well. You've mastered this new normal."

"I don't know if I'd say that I've mastered it, but I'm getting there. The classes at the foundation were unbelievably helpful. You won't believe this, but I'm learning to cook."

"No! Seriously?"

"One of my friends from the foundation is moving into my neighborhood soon. She's a terrific cook and is going to teach me how to make some of her favorites."

"I just watched Season 3 of *Master Chef*. That's the one Christine Ha won."

"The blind woman?"

"Yes. She opened my eyes to what you can do. I had no idea."

Emily laughed. "I'm not at her level."

"Knowing you, you will be, Em." He picked up his phone and began tapping on the screen.

"What are you doing?" Emily asked.

"I just ordered her cookbook for you. It says you'll have it Tuesday."

"You didn't have to do that." Emily sipped her coffee.

"I want you to have it. I want you to have everything you need, Em. I always have. When you had the accident—when you lost your sight—I had no idea what to do or how to help you."

"It was an incredibly challenging time for both of us. I see that now." She set her cup on the table.

"I wanted to be there for you, but it seemed like everything I did was wrong. I was only making matters worse."

"Your parents weren't there for you, growing up. You had no role models showing you how to be nurturing."

"I retreated into the only thing I feel like I'm definitely good at—my job. And making money. I wanted to be able to buy you everything you would need. I thought you'd have to stay home to be safe. I'd have to be the sole breadwinner."

"I never wanted that. I love what I do—you knew that."

He leaned his elbows on the table and rested his head in his hands. "It terrified me, thinking of you being out there—in the world—without being able to see." He played with the plastic lid on his cup, pulling it on and off. "I keep worrying about you getting lost and ..."

"Stop, Connor." Emily thrust out a hand. "I ... can't think about that," she snapped.

He waited for her to continue.

She responded slowly, choosing her words carefully. "Getting lost ... I ..." She turned her head aside. "I got myself here, didn't I?"

"Of course you did," he said.

"I'm well aware of the scary things that could happen to me, Connor. If I sat in my apartment and thought about them all the time, I'd never venture out. I refuse to let fear rule my life."

"I didn't mean to upset you."

"I'm not upset."

"Something's bothering you, Em. Do you want to tell me about it?"

"There's nothing to tell." She closed her eyes against the memory of the recent night when she'd left home without Garth. She cleared her throat. "You were talking about my job. I'm able to do it as well as I did before. I'm even better at some aspects of it now that I'm taking in data verbally and through my fingertips. If you'd have gone to the family sessions at the foundation, you would have learned all of this."

"I can see that. I'm sorry that I didn't."

Emily brought her cup to her lips and took another sip.

"How did you like Tokyo?"

"It's an exciting city. I think you'd like it. Maybe I can take you there one day." He took a deep breath and continued. "Being there—without you—allowed me to think clearly about my life. I still want to build a life with you. Being part of the couple that was us is at the center of everything I want."

"So, you came back."

"Yes. I realized that I couldn't win you back, long distance. I needed to be here. I had to see you. Being so far away from you has been torture."

Emily swirled the liquid in her cup.

"You've come so far. I'm proud of you, Em. You're even more amazing than I thought you were." He cleared his throat and continued. "Did you ... miss me?"

"I was so busy, learning how to function in my life again,

that I didn't have time to think about anyone else. I know that sounds selfish, but it's true." Emily drew a sharp breath. "And what about Gina? What about your feelings for her?"

"Oh … Em. I've never had any feelings for Gina. Not like that. I was drunk and feeling hurt and rejected. I was totally confused." His voice cracked. "If I could take back that kiss, I would. It was the stupidest ten seconds of my life." He continued in a rush. "None of it was Gina's fault. You need to believe me. I know it's caused a huge rift in your friendship. That's one of the worst things about it—I tore your best friend from you when you needed her most. The whole thing was inexcusable—and completely my fault. Don't blame Gina. She's a victim, just like you are. If you can't forgive me, I'll understand that. I had to come back to find out."

He tilted his head to the table, and they sat in silence.

Emily reached over and put a hand on top of his. "The months after the accident were a horrible time for us. We both faced enormous adjustments. I know that I was focused only on myself—and my needs."

"That was understandable."

"Even so, marriage always has two people in it. I wasn't thinking of you."

"That's incredibly generous of you, Em." His tone was hoarse with emotion. "Does this mean you'll give us a second chance?"

She pursed her lips. "Let's see each other again. See how it goes."

"Of course! I'd love that. Next weekend?"

"That works. Call me mid-week, and we'll set something up. And now, I'd better go. Thanks for the coffee." She reached for her wallet. "I'll leave the tip."

"You don't have to do that," Connor said.

"Have you started carrying cash?"

"Well … no."

Emily took a folded bill from her wallet.

"How do you know how much you're leaving on the table?"

"See how this bill is folded in half widthwise? That means it's a ten-dollar bill. The American Foundation for the Blind has a bill

folding protocol that bank tellers follow when they're giving paper money to blind people."

"That's so interesting. I never knew. Makes sense since all of our currency is the same size and color."

"Exactly. United States currency isn't accessible to the visually impaired. I can also use an app on my phone to identify the denomination of a bill. And I have a little device—the size of a credit card—that I can use to mark bills in braille."

"Wow. I can't believe I never thought about this."

"You'll be amazed—other than driving a car or flying an airplane, I can do everything you can do, Connor."

She dropped the bill on the table, grasped Garth's harness, and stood. They followed Connor onto the sidewalk.

"You'll hear from me on Wednesday." He touched her elbow and leaned toward her.

She didn't turn away.

Connor kissed her on the cheek.

She lingered, with her face touching his.

A man exiting the coffee shop said, "Excuse me," and they stepped apart.

"Have a good week," Emily said before she and Garth headed for home.

CHAPTER 30

$\mathcal{E}$mily and Garth rounded the corner from the elevator and set off down the long hallway toward Emily's office.

Garth continued along the familiar path. His tail began to wag at an increasing rate.

"You see something up there, don't you, boy? Or is it someone?"

"Hi, Emily."

"Good morning, Dhruv." He was standing at the door to her office. Garth led them past him, and Emily put her purse in a

drawer and her satchel in its usual spot under her desk. "Were you waiting for me?"

"Yes." He followed her into her office and hovered by her desk.

"What's up? Is there a problem with the solution we sent out Friday afternoon?"

"No. It's good. Everything's fine." He was shifting from

foot to foot.

"Okay. Well, then, what can I do for you?"

"Did she say anything about me?"

Emily rocked back in her chair. After seeing Connor yesterday

afternoon, she'd forgotten that she was going to find out for Stephanie what Dhruv thought of her. A smile spread across her face. This was going to be easy.

"She enjoyed meeting you."

"Did she think I was nice?"

"She already knew that based upon all the things I'd already told her."

"That's good." He paused. "It is good, isn't it?"

"Very good. Did you like her?"

Dhruv nodded his head emphatically. "She seemed nice."

"She's become a good friend of mine. I'm happy she's moving nearby."

"She's pretty, too. Very pretty. I think she's about my age."

"I'd guess so, yes."

"Is she smart? My family always tells me I should have someone smart. Because I'm so smart."

Emily couldn't suppress another smile. "I think Stephanie can keep up with you intellectually, Dhruv."

"Good. That's very good." He began to back towards her door.

"Are you going to ask her out?"

"Maybe," he said, and his breathing came faster. "I don't know.

I have to figure it out."

"What do you have to figure out?"

"Where to take her—what to do."

"You can go out to dinner—that's a common first date."

"Neither of us is a very 'common' person," Dhruv said quietly. "It's important for the first date to be unique. I've read that on lots of websites."

"You research dating?" Emily asked and knew the answer before he responded. Dhruv researched everything.

"I need to make an impression," he said with conviction. "I watch TV about it too. I've got to come up with something special."

Tears pricked the backs of Emily's eyes. Not many men were as thoughtful and considerate of others as Dhruv. She blinked hard. "You will, Dhruv. I'll think about it, too. I'll let you know if I come up with any ideas."

"That's good," he said. "We've got a plan." He turned to leave.

"One more thing, Dhruv. Don't wait until you've come up with what you think is perfect. I have a feeling that Stephanie will have a wonderful time with you, no matter what you do."

"Nope. That's not how I've read this works." His voice trailed off as he headed for his office. "I'm going to find the perfect date."

CHAPTER 31

*E*mily's phone quacked like a duck at seven o'clock, on the dot, Wednesday night. She grinned. Zoe had set up her phone to announce incoming calls this way. She'd meant to change it to something more professional sounding, but it always made her smile, so she'd left the setting as it was.

"It sounds like you're laughing," Connor said. "Am I interrupting something?"

"No—not at all. How are you?"

"It's Wednesday evening—I think the evening starts at seven —don't you agree?"

"I do. It is now officially evening."

"We said we'd figure out what we wanted to do this week-end. Are we still on? I'm hoping you haven't reconsidered."

"I'm still available," she said. "I'll need to spend most of the weekend studying braille, but I can take a break."

"I'm open and at your disposal. What do you have in mind?"

"I'm a night owl, as you know. I do my best studying after dinner. Let's do something in the afternoon."

"It's supposed to be nice on Saturday. Why don't I pick you up at eleven? We can grab an early lunch and then take a walk on one of the trails overlooking the ocean. I'll bet Garth would love that, too."

"I'm sure he would. I haven't walked near the ocean since ..." Her voice trailed off as she thought back to their honeymoon horseback ride, her fall on the beach, the day she lost her sight.

"Is this a bad idea? We can do something else."

"I think it's a brilliant idea. As you say, Garth will love it. Thank you for suggesting it."

"We can always change our minds, too. Do something else."

"Spontaneously change a plan? This is a new Connor," she teased.

"Old dogs can learn new tricks, as it turns out."

"What're you doing now?" Emily asked.

"I'm still at work. Settling into my new position. How about you?"

"Studying my braille. I'm enjoying it."

"That sounds like you."

"I've got to get back to it. I'll let you go."

"See you Saturday, Em. Thank you."

"For what?"

"For being brave enough to give us a second chance." He disconnected the call.

Emily rested her phone against her chin. Was that what she was doing—being brave? Or was she being incredibly foolish? She sighed heavily. Time would tell. Right now, she needed to return to her studies.

CHAPTER 32

*E*mily propped her feet up on the coffee table and sank back against the sofa cushions. It had been a busy week at work, and she wasn't in the mood to study. It was Friday night, after all. She tapped the screen of her phone and commanded it to call her mother. She was ready to tell her that she'd be seeing Connor the next day—and hear her mother's reaction to this revelation.

"Hi, sweetie," came the familiar voice. "I was just about to call you."

"Oh? What's up? Did Irene come home today, as planned?"

"No. They decided to keep her. She's not coming along as fast as they thought she would. She's very unsteady on her feet and can't be left alone."

"That's not good."

"I offered to have her come home to my house, but they wouldn't allow it. She needs more help than I can provide."

"What do they say about her prognosis? Should we be worried?"

"They said everybody reacts differently, and some people take more time than others to heal. Everything went well with the surgery. We just have to be patient."

"How's Irene feeling about it?"

"She's disappointed but determined not to let it get her down. She's taking it in stride."

"That figures. How's Zoe?"

"Zoe is another matter. She doesn't say much, but I know she's scared. She did fine during the week because she was busy with school, but this weekend's going to be hard. I just wish she had some friends in the neighborhood to play with." Martha sighed heavily. "I thought I'd take her to a movie, and we can walk Sabrina. What are you up to this weekend?"

Emily hesitated before responding. Before she could stop herself, Emily heard herself saying, "I thought I'd spend the weekend with the two of you." Connor would have to wait. Zoe needed her right now. And so did her mother.

"Oh, Em," Martha said. "That's such good news. Zoe will be thrilled. Don't you have other things to do?"

"I've got no plans, other than studying braille," Emily lied. "I'll bring my study materials with me."

"We can come in and pick you up in the morning."

"Nope. That's a long drive. I'll take a rideshare."

"Are you sure?"

"Positive."

"I'm going to hit the hay shortly. I'll be out first thing."

"Do you want to tell Zoe? She's in the tub but should be out any minute."

Emily leaned forward and pushed herself to her feet. She needed to busy herself, packing up the things she and Garth would need for a weekend away. "You can tell her. I've got a few things to attend to here. I'll see you first thing."

"Thank you, honey."

"Sweet dreams, Mom," Emily said before disconnecting the call. She stood, slapping her phone against her hand. How should she break the news to Connor that she wouldn't be able to see him as planned?

A wave of fatigue washed over her, and she yawned. Packing up and going to bed early was very appealing. She didn't have the energy to talk to Connor.

Emily dictated a text message to him: "Mom needs me to spend the weekend with her. Nothing serious, but it is urgent. I'll explain when I see you. Sorry for the short notice. Can I have a rain check?"

Satisfied, she tapped the send button and heard the telltale *whoosh.*

Emily spent the next half hour pulling together her clothes and toiletries for the weekend. She was about to scoop out enough food for Garth when her phone pinged twice.

She tapped the screen. The first text was from Connor, telling her that he understood and hoped everything was all right with Martha. He asked if they could reschedule for the following weekend.

Emily bit her lip. She'd wait to see how things went this weekend with Zoe before she responded to him. She still wasn't sure she wanted to go to a beach again.

The second message was from Gina. She listened as the phone read Gina's message. "Hi, Em. I'm going to be near your mom's tomorrow morning. If there's anything you'd like me to pick up for her—or if you have something you'd like to get to her—I'd be happy to be your delivery service. I'm leaving here early—about seven. Sorry for the short notice. Let me know. Smiley face emoji."

Emily smiled and turned back to Garth's dog food. Gina was

always thoughtful. She was closing the Ziplock bag full of kibble when the thought struck her. She pursed her lips and inhaled slowly. *Why not?* she thought. It wouldn't hurt to ask.

She responded to Gina's text. "I'm headed to Mom's tomorrow to spend the weekend. Would you mind if I rode along?"

Gina's response came flying back. "Are you kidding me? I'd love that! I'll pick you up at seven."

"Garth is coming with me. Is that okay?"

"Of course it is!"

"We'll be waiting out front." She supplied her address. "Can we stop for coffee on the way out of town? My treat."

"Now that's an offer I can't refuse. See you in the morning."

Emily hummed as she finished her tasks, took Garth outside, and crawled into bed. She and Gina had some tall fences to mend, but the warmth in her heart told her it might be possible.

CHAPTER 33

*E*mily and Garth stepped out into the foggy morning at five minutes before seven. She had a backpack containing her laptop and study materials, a crossbody bag that served as her purse and a small, wheeled suitcase.

Gina had arrived five minutes earlier, not wanting her friend to have to wait and was idling at the curb. She leapt out of her car and came to Emily's side. "Let me get your suitcase," she said. "I'll put it in the trunk."

"Thanks," Emily said. She put Garth into the backseat while Gina stowed her suitcase. "Can you believe we're both up and out before seven on a Saturday morning?"

"I know," Gina replied as they got into the car. "Since when did we become early birds?"

"Mom will be shocked when we drive up," Emily said. "Why are you going to the old stomping grounds this weekend?"

"My mom and dad are taking that extended trip to Europe that they always talked about, and I'm looking after their house —watering the plants and bringing in the mail."

"I'm so happy to hear that they're finally doing it. After your mom's breast cancer, I didn't know if ..."

"I know. Thank God they caught it early. She's completely recovered. Their trip got delayed and not canceled."

Gina turned off the road into the drive-through lane of the national chain coffee shop. "Your usual?" she asked.

"You remember?"

Gina scoffed. She rolled down her window and placed their order. "Did I get yours right?"

"To the letter," Emily said. Her voice carried her smile. "Are you spending the weekend, too?"

"No. Craig and I are headed to a little inn on the coast. Sort of a mini-vacation. He's had it planned for weeks. That's why I needed to do this early. He's picking me up at eleven thirty."

"That sounds very romantic. You like this guy, don't you?"

"I do. I've never felt so comfortable with anyone in my whole life. It's like he 'gets' me. I can be myself."

"I'm happy for you, Gina. Truly, I am."

"Not many people get to feel this way," Gina said. "I always thought that's the way you and Connor felt about each other."

"I thought that at one time, too," Emily said and turned her face to the window.

"I'm sorry, Em. I shouldn't have mentioned him."

"It's okay." She faced forward. "I've actually been talking to Connor again. He's back in town."

"Really. Is he here on business?"

"No. He took a lateral move to get reassigned to the San Francisco office. He said he came home to see if we could work things out. He wants to salvage our marriage."

"Oh, Em. I'm so glad to hear this. You guys never had a chance to make a go of it."

Emily remained silent, sipping her coffee.

The windshield wipers clicked as they cleared the fog.

"How do you feel about his being back? Are you … willing …?"

"To forgive and forget?"

"Em … I don't know what to say. I'm so sorry. Nothing happened between us, and nothing *would* have happened." She put on her blinker and pulled off the highway at the next exit. Gina turned into the large, deserted parking lot of a big box store that wouldn't open for several hours. She put the car in park and swiveled to face Emily.

"We needed to have this conversation at some point. Are you ready to hear me out?"

Emily stiffened but nodded. "Now's as good a time as any."

"I was with Connor frequently when you were at Martha's, taking classes at the foundation. All of our conversations were about you. The only thing Connor wanted to talk about was you. You were his sole focus. He felt sad and frustrated and inadequate."

Emily shifted in her seat.

"He blamed himself for cajoling you into going on that damned horseback ride. He takes full responsibility for your fall and retinal detachments."

"It wasn't his fault. I chose to get on that horse. It was a freak accident."

"He didn't think you felt that way at the time."

Emily brought her hands to her cheeks. "I did blame him—at first. I was so mad—mostly at myself, but also at him. I knew it wasn't fair at the time, but I was shocked and depressed."

"He sensed all of that, Em. He was inconsolable. From my perspective—as a friend to you both—I felt like you were each drowning in different pools. I wanted to throw life preservers to you both, but I couldn't figure out how to get to either of you." Gina began to cry.

"I was so focused on myself, I didn't think of any of you."

"Who could blame you?" Gina choked. "We all would have done the same."

"I was lucky. I have my mom, and Connor and you. Plus Dhruv—and my coworkers. You all brought me back."

Gina began rummaging in her purse.

Emily opened her crossbody bag and handed Gina a purse-sized package of tissues.

"Thanks," Gina managed through sobs.

"I've never known you to have a tissue when you needed one," Emily said.

"I always had you for that."

Both women chuckled.

"Connor was drunk, and that kiss wasn't directed at me—it was more a release of frustration. With himself. He was never interested in me. I needed you to hear that from me."

They sat in silence; the car cocooned by the fog.

"Connor told me as much," Emily said.

"He did?"

"We had coffee last weekend. We were going to go hiking this afternoon, but I had to come home."

"Is anything wrong with Martha?"

"No. She's fine. Her neighbor is in the hospital, and Mom's keeping Irene's granddaughter for her until she gets out. Zoe and I are close, so I decided I'd spend the weekend with her."

"Is that the little girl that got so sick with Reye's syndrome? You went to the hospital all by yourself to see her?"

"How'd you know about that?"

"Martha told me. We were all so worried about you."

"In many ways, Zoe saved my life," Emily said. "I owe it to

her to make her feel better if I can. I can see Connor another time."

"I hope you do. I've always thought the two of you were made for each other."

"We'll see," Emily said. "I agree that we need to find out." She tapped the screen on her phone. The read-out informed them it was eight o'clock.

"We'd better get going if you're going to get back in time for your big date."

Gina started the car, then reached across the console and clasped Emily's hand. "I'm so glad that we cleared the air. Part of me wishes that I could spend the weekend with you, like the old days."

"Your romantic getaway sounds like much more fun than listening to music or poking around the mall." Emily squeezed her hand back. "Promise you'll tell me all about it."

"Only if you promise me you'll reschedule with Connor."

"Deal," Emily said, releasing Gina's hand.

Gina put the car in gear, and they resumed their journey.

CHAPTER 34

*I*t was Saturday. At least, I thought it was Saturday. Emily had ordered in a pizza last night. That's what we always did on Friday nights. Why in the world was she up so early? Didn't we sleep in on the weekend?

It wasn't up to me to question our plans. My life was all in the implementation. I lifted my hindquarters into the air and stretched, doing my best downward dog pose.

Emily was all business when she took me outside, so I didn't dally. We must be going to the office, I thought. Emily was always doing big, smart things. I knew she was the smartest of them all.

I was curious when she clutched a rolling suitcase on her right side, with me leading the way on her left. I was puzzled that a car was waiting for us, and a young, blonde woman I recognized got out and greeted Emily. She was the woman I'd smelled at the cosmetic counter. Emily's friend Gina.

I hopped in the backseat, as directed, and tried to get our

bearings out the window. The fog was too thick, and I soon succumbed to the futility of my efforts.

I settled onto the floor of the car and stayed there until we suddenly turned off the road, and the car began to inch along.

Gina rolled her window down and answered questions emanating from a voice in the box next to her window. She pulled forward and took two paper cups from a pair of hands leaning out of a window. She handed one to Emily.

I tensed and put my nose in the air. Caramel macchiato with an extra shot of espresso and no whip. Just like Emily liked. I relaxed and put my head on my paws.

The car started to move again, gaining speed. The windshield wipers clapped rhythmically. Gina and Emily began to talk softly. My lids grew heavy.

The next thing I knew, the car stopped. Emily and Gina were facing each other. Neither made a move to get out of the vehicle. I could feel the energy flowing between them; I could sense the raw emotion rising to the surface. Unless I missed my mark, one of them was going to cry.

I rested my muzzle on the console between the front seats and shifted my gaze between the two women. I could always jump up and tend to them if necessary. Exuberant doggie kisses never failed to bring an end to an uncomfortable situation. I knew that dog pheromones were calming and remembered that some of my classmates from the Guide Dog Center trained as therapy dogs for PTSD. I could handle whatever was going to transpire between them.

Gina began to cry.

I raised up onto my front haunches, preparing to make my move. Just then, Emily reached into her purse and extended something to Gina. There was kindness in that gesture. I waited and watched.

They continued to talk, and soon, both of them laughed.

I eased back but continued to watch them. I didn't know what they had said, but there was a sea change in the feeling between them. It was like they'd crested the top of a hill after an arduous climb and were now on the grassy downward slope.

They clasped hands, then Gina started the car again. She winked at me in the rearview mirror, and we were on our way.

I liked this Gina. If she and my Emily were going to be friends,

it was fine by me.

CHAPTER 35

$\mathcal{M}$artha drew Gina close and hugged her. "It's wonderful to see you, dear. It was so nice of you to give Emily a ride."

"I wish you could stay," Zoe said.

"She has to get back. She has a big date," Emily said in a stage whisper.

"I wish she could come with us," Zoe said. "It'd be fun."

"Why? Where are we going?" Emily asked. "What have you two got cooked up?"

"We're going clothes shopping," Zoe said. "For you. We're going to buy you pretty tops—not just black."

"Oh ... we don't need to do that ..." Emily sputtered.

"You said you wanted to," Zoe said. "When we were getting your new makeup."

"I think that's a great idea," Gina said. "If I didn't have plans, I'd love to tag along. I've been telling this one," she pointed to Emily, "for years that she needed to spice up her wardrobe."

"All right, all right," Emily said. "The stores won't be open this early. We'll go as soon as they are."

"Perfect," Gina said. She turned to Zoe. "Will you text me photos of what you pick out? I'd love to see."

Zoe nodded her head vigorously.

"I'd better be going. It'll take me half an hour at Mom and Dad's, and then I need to head back."

"Thank you, Gina. For the ride and … everything."

Gina sniffed. "You're welcome, Em. I'm so glad we got to talk."

"Have fun this weekend. Give me a call next week?" Emily asked.

"You bet," Gina said before turning and walking to her car.

***

"It's time to head out," Martha said, grabbing her purse as the doorbell rang. "Who in the world could that be?" She moved to the door and peered through the peephole, suddenly stepping back and throwing the door open.

"Gina! What on earth are you doing here?"

Emily, Garth, and Zoe joined Martha.

"I suddenly have time to go shopping with you guys. If I'm still invited?"

"Yes!" Zoe cried.

"What happened?" Emily asked. "Is everything all right?"

"One of the other doctors called in sick, so Craig had to go in to cover office hours. He's a veterinarian. Did I tell you that?"

"No."

"That's cool!" Zoe said.

"Are you still going?"

"Yes, but he has to work until three—which usually means

four. He said he'll pick me up by four thirty, and we can still make our seven-thirty dinner reservation."

"You came back to join us!" Martha said, giving Gina a hug.

"What better way to fill my time than shopping with you three?"

"Indeed," Martha said. "We were just leaving."

"I'll drive," Gina said. "I still remember the way to the mall. I think Emily and I spent the best part of our high school years there."

***

Emily ran her hand along the bar in the dressing room. "There must be at least fifty hangers on this bar," she said. "Do I really need to try on all of these?"

"Yes," came the response, in unison, from her three companions. The salesclerk had placed them in the largest dressing room and had brought in two additional chairs so all three of them could sit.

"Sorry, boy," Emily said to Garth. "Make yourself comfortable. This is going to take a while."

"Do I need to remind you that, back in the day, you'd have thought nothing of trying on fifty shirts?"

"Fifty for each of us," Emily said, pulling her T-shirt off. "And sometimes we wouldn't even buy anything. I'll bet the salesclerks hated us."

"At least we always hung everything back up." Gina turned to Martha. "We never left a dressing room in a mess. You and my mom taught us to be considerate."

Martha beamed. "I love hearing that."

"What colors do I have here?"

Zoe jumped to her feet. "We've got mostly blues, greens, and yellows. I picked out a pink one, too."

"Is it the same color as your favorite shirt?"

"Yep."

"Let's try that one on first. Can you help me with that, Zoe?"

Zoe slid hangers across the rod until she found what she was looking for. She removed the pink top from the hanger and handed it to Emily.

Emily inserted her head and arms in the knitted top and pulled it down to her hips. She felt the placement of the shoulder seams and smoothed the garment across her hips. "It seems like it fits. What do you think?"

"It's your size," Martha said. "Fits like a glove."

"I love the color on you," Gina said. "Some redheads can't wear pink, but this shade looks beautiful on you."

Zoe bounced on her toes.

Emily pulled the shirt back over her head. "We're getting this one." She handed it to Zoe. "Can you put the ones we're keeping in a separate pile?"

"Here—I'll hold them," Martha said, taking the tops from Zoe.

"Can you hand me each shirt to try on—just like you did this one, Zoe?"

They began moving through the mound of clothes. Emily was pleased that she could accurately assess the fit of a garment by how it felt under her hands.

Zoe handed Martha the keepers and rehung the items that would go back on the rack.

"You're doing a terrific job, Zoe," Gina said. "Everything's rehung so nicely. You're as good as any personal shopper I've ever worked with."

Zoe flushed. Her gaze darted from Gina to Martha.

"A personal shopper is someone who helps you find the best clothes for yourself," Martha explained.

"Do you have one? A personal shopper?" Zoe asked Gina.

"I do," Gina says. "It saves so much time, and I always know I look good in whatever I buy."

"That sounds very fancy," Zoe said, handing Emily another garment.

"Maybe you'll be one when you grow up," Gina said.

"I want to invent things," Zoe said.

"That's very cool," Gina said. "What would you like to invent?"

"Devices to help blind people," Zoe said.

Emily stopped pulling a sweater over her head.

"Or ice cream flavors. I can't decide which."

Gina laughed. "Those are essential things. You'd be great at both of them."

"I've noticed that when Zoe puts her mind to anything, she does it very well," Martha said. She shifted her weight in her chair. "There's only one more thing to try."

Zoe handed Emily the last garment.

"This fabric feels slippery and almost metallic. It's heavy, too. And long. What is this?"

"It's an emerald green cocktail dress," Martha said. "I picked it out for you."

"It's gorgeous, Em," Gina interjected. "A shimmery sheath. So classy."

Emily held the dress out to Zoe. "I'm not going to try this on. Why in the world would I need a cocktail dress?"

Zoe kept her hands at her sides. "It's beautiful. I think you should try it on."

Emily kept her face turned to the three other females in the dressing room. "Seriously?"

"Just try it," Martha said. "For me."

Emily pulled the dress over her head and pushed her hands into the sleeves.

Her audience gasped in unison.

"Oh, Em," Gina breathed. "That dress fits you like it was custom made. You look stunning."

"I agree, honey," Martha said, her voice hoarse with emotion.

"Why would I buy this? I'm never going to wear it."

"You won't wear it if you don't buy it," Zoe chimed in.

The three women laughed.

"You'll wear it, honey. I know you will. Buy it as an affirmation of your belief in your happy future," Martha said.

It was Emily's turn to get choked up. "Oh, all right." She carefully wriggled out of the dress and held it out to Martha. "How many did we decide to get?" Emily asked.

Martha counted the pile of tops on her lap. "Twelve."

"I don't need that many," Emily said.

"Since when has need had anything to do with it? You wanted new tops, and the shopping gods were smiling on you today. You found eleven that you like, plus the most amazing dress you've ever owned. The color is stunning on you. When was the last time that happened to you?" Gina asked.

Emily shrugged.

"Remember how we used to say that if either of us had a day where everything fit—the store carried everything in our size— that we would buy it all?"

Emily took the shirt she'd worn into the store from Zoe. "I vaguely remember saying something like that."

"Well, that's where we are, right now. Everything looked fabulous on you. Seize the moment."

"Okay, okay," Emily said. "Enough. I'll get them all." She turned to Zoe. "I have braille color tags at my apartment that I can sew into these garments to identify them. Will you help me with that the next time you come to see me?"

"Yep," replied the little girl.

"Let's head to the register and have this rung up," Martha said. "When we're done, I'd like to take the best team of shoppers out to lunch. Zoe—you get to choose the restaurant."

"The pretzel place that puts hot dogs in the middle?

That's my favorite."

"Mine, too," Gina said. "And the next time I need new clothes, I want the three of you to go with me. What do you say, Zoe?"

The little girl wiggled with excitement. "That'd be so fun."

"I'll lead the way," Martha said as the group of females and the handsome black dog made their way out of the dressing room. A delighted salesclerk processed the sale, and the register was clunking out the receipt in no time.

Gina took the shopping bag from the clerk, and the three generations of women left the store.

CHAPTER 36

"Can we let Garth and Sabrina make friends?" Zoe asked from the backseat where she sat, patting Garth at her feet.

"I think that's a great idea," Emily said. "When we get home, I'll take Garth through the side gate to the backyard. You can go inside and put Sabrina on her leash and then bring her out."

"Okay."

"We'll walk them, on their leashes, past each other—about ten feet apart."

"Why?"

"We'll see how they react. Garth has been trained to ignore other dogs, but he did get attacked by a phony service dog in a restaurant when he was young. His puppy raisers told me about it. He may be hesitant. And Sabrina won't know how to behave. We'll want to make sure she's not feeling scared."

"How will we know? She tugs on the leash and barks when we meet other dogs on our walks."

"Does she snap or try to bite them?"

"No. She's always wagging her tail, and if the other owner lets them say hello, she's fine."

"Tail wagging is always a good sign," Emily said. "Look at her ears, too. If they're pinned back, that tells you she's upset."

"Got it. So, we'll walk them past each other and watch them."

"If they seem okay, we'll let them get close, and we'll take it from there."

Gina pulled into the driveway.

Zoe dashed out of the car. "I'm gonna get Sabrina right now." Martha followed her and unlocked the front door.

"I wish I could stay to see how the dogs get along, but I have to get home to get ready."

"I'll let you know how it goes," Emily said. "Thank you for coming back and going shopping with us."

"It was fun. Like old times."

"It really was. Let me know how your weekend goes," Emily said.

"I'll call you this week. What night works for you?"

"I'm anxious to hear. How about Monday?"

A smile flooded Gina's face. "Monday it is."

Emily opened her car door. "I have a feeling a certain little girl and her miniature schnauzer are already out back, waiting for us."

"I'd put money on it. Enjoy the rest of your weekend. I'll talk to you soon."

CHAPTER 37

For some reason, we weren't going in the front door. If Emily wanted to go around the side of Martha's garage and through the gate to the backyard, so be it.

Zoe was waiting for us. She clutched a leash attached to a small dog with an elaborate haircut. The dog crouched, then sprang up and began to wiggle as we came into view.

I kept my eyes front and center. I was in my harness and still on duty. I didn't have time for such frivolity.

"Zoe?" Emily called.

"We're over here," Zoe replied.

"I'm going to remove Garth's harness," Emily said. "That way, he'll know he's not working. This will be play time for him."

"Got it."

Emily slipped my harness off over my head and snapped open her cane that she'd withdrawn from her backpack. We turned to her right. "We're going to walk this way, toward you," she called over her shoulder.

"And I walk the other way, so we cross in the middle. I keep going."

"That's right. Ten feet apart. Don't let Sabrina pull you over to us."

"I won't," Zoe said in a serious tone. "Sabrina, heel," she said.

We walked past each other. I cut my eyes to observe Sabrina. She tried to lunge toward me, but Zoe corrected her.

We repeated the process several more times. I wagged my tail on the last pass.

"Sabrina's wagging her tail," Zoe called. "Garth's wagged his, too."

Emily stopped walking. Zoe did the same.

"What's Sabrina doing right now?"

"She's got her front legs on the ground, with her butt in the air. She's wagging her tail so hard she's about to knock herself over."

Emily chuckled. "I can picture that. Let's walk toward each other to see if they want to get acquainted. Don't drop your leash! If Sabrina gets aggressive, you'll need to pull her back."

"I won't let her hurt Garth."

Emily took a step toward Zoe and Sabrina. I accompanied her at a dignified pace. Everything about Sabrina's body language told me she was friendly, but I was still wary of dogs from outside the guide community.

I had nothing to worry about. Sabrina bounded over to me. She sniffed my face, her nose pulsing like a blender on high speed. She continued along my body.

I turned my head to her, giving her the same treatment. We were soon examining each other's most intimate parts in the way that dogs do.

My tail was wagging almost as fast as Sabrina's.

"I think we can take their leashes off," Emily said, unclipping mine from my collar.

Zoe followed suit.

Sabrina crouched into a downward dog pose and touched her nose to mine before taking off across the yard at a gallop. I followed and soon caught up with her. I had to give her credit— she was fast—but she was no match for my long strides.

Emily held out her arm to Zoe, and Zoe stepped into her.

They stood, together, in the afternoon sunshine, watching us zoom by them.

"They're having fun, aren't they?"

"Yes! I can't believe how fast they can run," Zoe said.

"Garth rarely gets the chance to stretch his legs like this."

"I knew they'd get along," Zoe said.

Sabrina and I veered left at the last minute to avoid colliding with our humans as Zoe leaned against Emily, and Emily put her arm across Zoe's shoulders.

"They're friends," I heard Zoe say. "I'll bet they'll be best friends."

I liked the sound of that.

Emily tightened her arm around the little girl. "Yes. Just like us."

I liked the sound of that even better.

CHAPTER 38

"She's asleep," Martha said, sinking into the sofa next to Emily and stretching her legs out in front of her. She raised a hand to cover a yawn. "This week has reminded me how much energy little girls and dogs have."

A faint, rumbling snore rose from under the coffee table.

"I think Garth feels the same way," Emily said. "That run in the backyard with Sabrina took it out of him."

"I watched from the kitchen window. It looked like you were having a great time."

"We were," Emily said.

"What do you want to do tonight?" Martha yawned again.

"I thought I'd call Connor," Emily said. "Then I need to study my braille."

Martha's eyebrows shot up. "Call Connor?"

"Yeah. I've been wanting to talk to you about that."

Martha swiveled to her daughter.

"You know that he left me a note. That's why you encouraged me to check my mailbox on that Sunday when you came to pick up Zoe."

"I ran into him when he was coming out of your building."

"You never told me that you talked to him."

"He wanted me to put in a good word with you. I told him I wasn't going to interfere." She inhaled, then continued. "I was wondering if you'd ever read that note. I figured you'd tell me about it when you were ready."

"Thanks for giving me space, Mom. I did read it and then ran into him in my hallway. He was leaving lilacs for me on the anniversary of our first date."

"That was nice."

Emily nodded. "We met for coffee, and I agreed to see him again. We were going to take a hike this afternoon."

"Are you considering getting back together?"

"I don't know," Emily said. "Maybe. What I do know is that our marriage got off to the rockiest possible start. Neither of us was at our best. We never had a chance to succeed as a married couple."

"That's how it seemed to me, too."

"You like Connor, don't you, Mom?"

"I think he's a good man, and he loves you. Before you lost your sight, I thought you were perfectly suited for each other."

"And now?"

"I don't know. You've both changed."

"I need to find out. I think I want to give this marriage a try." Emily put her head in her hands. "Do you think I'm crazy to do this?"

"Not at all." Martha slid over and put her arm around her daughter's shoulders. "There's only one way to find out. I'm proud of you for being brave enough to face this."

Emily turned her head away from her mother. Was she

being brave? Her confidence in her ability to cope on her own had taken a nosedive in the days since she'd become lost in the fog. Was she viewing Connor as a crutch?

"Is there something else?" Martha asked.

If she were going to tell her mother about that terrifying night, now would be the time. But what good would that do? It would only worry her mother. There was no point in inflicting that on Martha. Emily had found the mailbox and made her way home. The trauma of that night would fade in time.

"Not a thing," Emily replied.

Martha squeezed her shoulders and placed a kiss on her daughter's temple before pushing herself into a standing position. "I'm going to put my pajamas on and get into bed and read until I fall asleep."

"Sweet dreams."

"Say hi to Connor for me."

CHAPTER 39

*C*onnor picked up on the first ring. "Em, I'm so glad to hear from you."

"Am I interrupting …?"

"Not at all. I'm sorting through a stack of resumes that I didn't have time to look at last week. I'm hiring two new sales managers."

"Working late on Saturday night?"

"Guilty as charged," he said. "Since I wasn't spending time with you, I thought I'd do something productive."

"You're a workaholic, Connor Harrington," she said.

"I'd hoped to be spending time with you, remember?"

"Fair enough. I'm not calling to chastise you. I wanted to apologize for canceling on such short notice."

"Don't worry about that," he replied. "How's Martha? Is everything okay?"

"Mom's fine. It's her next-door neighbor, Irene."

"She's the one who has her little granddaughter living with her. The girl who's taken such a shine to you?"

"Yes. And the girl's name is Zoe. Irene fell and broke her hip. Zoe—and her dog, Sabrina—have been staying with Mom. Irene was supposed to come home from the hospital on Friday but hasn't been recovering as quickly as they've hoped. She's gone to a rehabilitation hospital until she can function safely at home."

"That's unfortunate. Will she be okay?"

"Yes. She just needs more time. Zoe was pretty upset about it. She lives with her grandmother because her parents were killed in a car accident."

"That's tragic! Irene's being in the hospital must be doubly scary for her."

"It is. I talked to Mom on Friday night and decided to come down here to spend the weekend with them to cheer Zoe up."

"That's exactly what you should have done," Connor said.

"Really? You don't mind?"

"I'm disappointed that we didn't get to spend time together, but I completely understand. Have you three girls had fun together?"

"So much fun," Emily replied. "Thank you for being understanding, Connor."

"When are you coming back to the city?"

"Tomorrow afternoon."

"Do you need a lift?"

"I'll get a rideshare."

"How about I pick you up? Maybe we can grab dinner?"

"That's nice, but I'm not getting much studying done. Zoe and Mom have gone to bed, and I was going to work tonight, but I'm too tired. I need to get home and hit the books."

"My offer still stands—we can at least spend time together on the ride back."

"You don't mind? I take rideshares all the time."

"I hate to think of my … my wife in a stranger's car."

"It's fine, Connor. I'm perfectly safe out there, on my own. I always have Garth with me, too."

"I'm sure you are," he replied quickly. "I didn't mean to offend you. I'd still like to see you, that's all."

"If you don't mind coming all the way out here to get me, I'd appreciate that."

"Done. What time would milady like her chariot to arrive?"

"One thirty? I'd like to be on my way right after lunch."

"One thirty it is. I'll see you then."

"Thank you, again, Connor. I'll let you get back to your resumes."

"Sleep well, Em."

***

"That little girl idolizes you," Connor said as they pulled out of

Martha's driveway. He leaned forward and waved to the girl who stood on the porch, a furry white dog at her feet, staring forlornly

at the car.

"Zoe and I have a powerful connection. If it weren't for her, I wouldn't have found Garth." She paused before continuing in a somber tone. "She brought me out of my depression over you … and Gina."

Connor swallowed hard. "Then it seems I owe her a deep debt of gratitude."

They sat in silence as Connor accelerated onto the highway.

"Did you find any promising candidates in those resumes?"

"I've set aside four of them to interview. Nobody jumped out of the pack."

"What does your HR department think?"

"That they've sent me dozens of qualified candidates and that I'm far too picky."

Emily reached over to pat his arm. "Some things don't change."

"I don't want to hire the wrong person. Training someone who can't do the job is a waste of time."

"I agree," Emily said. "You've always been able to hire the best fit for a job. Listen to your gut. If HR has to find you more candidates to consider ... well ... that's their job."

"You think so?"

"I do."

"That means a lot to me. Sometimes I wonder if I'm just ... difficult."

"Demanding excellence isn't being difficult. Don't start doubting yourself."

"Thanks for your support." He relaxed back into his seat. "I've had an idea for next weekend."

"I thought we'd do the hike that we'd planned for yesterday but didn't get to do."

"We can still do that if you'd like. I looked at the seven-day forecast, and it's supposed to be rainy and cold."

"That's a bummer."

"I was wondering if you'd like to go to the symphony instead."

She whipped her head in his direction. "Really?"

"I know you love classical music."

"You hate the symphony."

"No, I don't." Connor cleared his throat. "I never really gave it a chance. I figured you'd enjoy it. Especially now."

"I'd love to go. Thank you very much."

"Perfect!" His voice was gleeful. "Tickets were going fast, so

I've already bought them. Just in case. The concert is at seven. Shall we do dinner before or after?"

"Let's be very chic and eat fashionably late."

"I was hoping you'd say that. Where would you like to go?"

"I'll leave that up to you. Surprise me."

"I'll pick a place that won't be too noisy. And I'll let the restaurant know that Garth will be coming. I know they can't legally turn us away because of him, but I don't want there to be any issues."

"You've done your homework."

"I'm learning all I can about the rights of people with visual impairments." He pulled to a stop outside of her apartment. "Home."

"That went fast." She got out of the car and reached for Garth, putting him back into his harness. "I can manage my stuff from here."

"Don't be silly. I know I'm not coming in, but I can carry your suitcase and all of those department store bags for you."

"You're always a gentleman, aren't you?"

"Always." He led the way to the elevator and down the hallway

to her apartment.

Garth stopped at her door.

"Thank you, again, Connor, for bringing us home."

"Do you need anything? Can I run to the store for you?"

Emily unlocked her door, and she and Garth stepped inside. "We're fine, but thank you for offering."

"Where do you want your suitcase and these shopping bags?"

"Just set them to the left of the door."

He did as she directed. "I'll pick you up on Saturday—at six."

"I'll look forward to it. How fancy do I need to dress?"

"I don't know. What would you like to do?"

Emily leaned against the door jam and tapped her finger on her teeth. "I think I'd like to go glam. I got some new clothes this weekend, including a fancy cocktail dress that Mom, Zoe, and Gina all insisted I buy. This will give me a chance to wear it."

He smiled broadly. "Good for them. Glam, it will be. I'll wear the custom-tailored suit I had made in Tokyo."

"Excellent."

"Well … I'd better let you go," he sighed heavily.

Emily felt him lean toward her. She turned her face to his and brushed her lips against his. She withdrew them quickly and stepped back. "See you soon," she said, then shut the door.

CHAPTER 40

*T*hank god he wasn't coming in. My mind needed to process what I'd just seen.

I headed straight for my water bowl.

Emily beat me to it. She rinsed and filled it with fresh, cool water.

I lapped greedily, sneezing loudly when I splashed water up my nose. When I was done, I headed for my bed.

I'd had a clear view of that scene at the door. Emily had definitely leaned in and kissed him. What, exactly, did that mean? Were we changing how we felt about him?

Emily was glad to see him when he'd arrived to pick us up. He was overjoyed to see her; that much was clear. His car's backseat was roomy and comfortable, and the leather seats were cool against my side. That was all in the plus column.

I'd never really liked the guy, but he seemed different now. I'd try to keep an open mind on the subject—for Emily's sake. Whatever made her happy made me happy, too.

Emily busied herself, taking all of the items out of the department store bags and placing them on hangers. She pushed all the new things to one side of her closet. "We'll put braille labels identifying the colors on all of these later," she said to me over her shoulder.

She held up a shiny garment in front of herself, her face visible behind the hanger. "What do you think, boy? Is it as fabulous as
they said it was?"

I thumped my tail. Anything that Emily wore was fabulous.

"Okay. Thanks for the confirmation." She hung the garment on
a high hook on the back of her closet door and joined me on my bed.

"It was a fun weekend, wasn't it, Garth? The best one I've had since … well … in a very long time. How about you? Did you like meeting Sabrina?" She kissed the top of my head and got to her feet. Before long, she was concentrating on her laptop and the braille keyboard attached to it.

I was still pondering her question. Had I had a fun weekend?

The answer to that was a definitive yes. I took stock. Riding in the car—two longer rides to Martha's and back and the trip to and
from the mall—was always on my list. Department stores were interesting, but the food court was an olfactory delight. The scent of baking bread from the pretzel place Zoe selected was almost thick enough to taste.

And then there were Zoe and Sabrina. I had grown very fond of that little girl and was relieved she had Sabrina to look after her. We'd had a talk about Zoe—Sabrina and I—at the water bowl after we'd finished our game of chase. Sabrina wasn't formally trained to take care of a person like I was, but she understood Zoe's emotional needs. She didn't know exactly what was wrong with the little girl's grandmother, but she knew Zoe was anxious about her. Sabrina had assured me she'd dispense all the doggy kisses that might be necessary.

I turned onto my side. Running like wild with Sabrina had been the highpoint of my weekend. I had the advantage of height, but that little dog was deceptively agile. She'd given me a run for my money.

As I drifted off to sleep, I thought about how much fun it would be to see her again.

CHAPTER 41

*E*mily placed Garth's bowl of kibble on the floor and turned to the turkey curry she'd picked up on the way home. She unwrapped the to-go utensils, grabbed an iced tea from her refrigerator, and took her meal to the coffee table. She settled herself onto the sofa and placed a call to Gina.

"Okay, spill the beans. I want to hear all about it."

Gina laughed. "Do you want all the details? There's a lot to tell."

"I just got home and fed Garth. I've got takeout for myself. Do you mind if I eat while I listen?"

"Not a bit. Turkey curry?"

"You know me so well. Quit stalling—tell." Emily speared a forkful of her dinner.

"Oh, Em. It was wonderful. The inn on the coast was beyond charming. It was tucked into trees on the top of a cliff. There wasn't a beach, but our room had the most beautiful view of the ocean."

"Sounds amazing."

"He picked me up a few minutes early, and we got to watch the sunset from our room before we went to dinner."

Gina grew silent.

"And?"

"Oh, Em. I'm sorry. Here I am describing things I can see ..."

"That I can't, anymore? Don't worry about that. I can experience those things in my own way. I can picture what you're describing."

"I don't know how to talk about this with you."

"You're doing fine. Blind people talk to each other about seeing things all the time. It's not a forbidden word. So... continue." She took another bite.

"We had the most delicious dinner at the inn, in the coziest restaurant. He had called ahead and ordered cherries jubilee for dessert."

"Yum! He's batting a thousand, so far."

"We slept in and had brunch on our terrace. He'd arranged for a late checkout, and on our way home, we drove along the coast and poked through a bunch of galleries and boutiques. You know the kinds of shops I'm talking about—where local artists display their work."

"You love doing that. Did he enjoy that?"

"He was the one who wanted to keep going from shop to shop."

"A man who loves to shop? He sounds perfect."

"You know—I think he is."

"He's also a romantic, to have planned all of this."

"That's just it—he's a very practical sort of person. This took real thought and effort on his part."

"Why this weekend? I know you; it wasn't your birthday." Emily took a drink of her iced tea.

"He said he wanted to get away and have a special weekend, just the two of us."

"There's something else," Emily said. "I can hear it in your voice."

"He told me he loves me, Em. We told each other."

"I'm so happy for you, Gina. You've waited so long for this."

"Maybe all those losers and creeps that I seemed to fall for were just keeping me off the market until Craig came along."

"He sounds like he's exactly the kind of man you deserve. I'm delighted for you, Gina."

"Thank you, Em. I'm glad that I got to tell you about him."

"I love hearing all of this." Emily set down her fork and pushed the empty takeaway container to one side. "I need to confess something to you," she said.

"What?" Gina's voice held a note of alarm.

"You were right about that dress."

"What dress? What're you talking about?"

"That fancy cocktail dress the three of you coerced me into buying."

"Really?"

"I'm going to wear it Saturday night."

"OMG—now it's your turn to tell."

"Connor and I are going to the symphony Saturday night and to dinner afterward."

"Your Connor?"

"Yep."

"How'd you talk him into that?"

"I didn't. It was his idea."

"Wow—I think he's trying to impress you."

"I guess."

"When did you decide this?"

"He gave me a ride home from Mom's yesterday afternoon."

"Now it's my turn to be pleased," Gina said. "I'm so happy to hear this. And you're going to look spectacular in that dress."

"Are you gloating?"

"Maybe a little bit," Gina confessed. "And now I'm going to have to call you next week to find out how *your* date went."

"It's a plan," Emily said. "Talk to you on Monday night."

CHAPTER 42

We'd both had baths in the afternoon. Emily had brushed my coat until even I knew it shined. She'd wrapped her auburn hair around a long cylinder that smelled hot, frequently cursing when she'd burned her fingers. Her hair now cascaded around her shoulders in long curls. I wore my green working harness, and she was in that shimmery dress she'd bought when we'd gone shopping with the girls. It matched the color of my harness. We looked sharp together.

Emily was swiping across her lips with a cylindrical object when we heard a knock on the door. She shoved the cylinder into a small bag and zipped it shut before crossing to answer the door.

Connor stood in the open doorway, carrying another bouquet of flowers. I lifted my nose, sniffed, and waited. No itching. No burning. Evidently, this bunch didn't contain lilacs.

"You look beautiful, Em! That dress is stunning."

"Thank you. Mom and Gina didn't lead me astray by insisting

I buy it?"

"Not at all. It looks like it was made for you."

Connor was looking sharp in a dark blue suit, white shirt, and

navy tie. I sidled closer to him. We'd spent a lot of time on my appearance, too. Maybe he would notice.

"Can I say hi to Garth? Or is he working?"

"He will be soon, but you can go ahead. I'll get my coat and purse."

"I brought you flowers," Connor said.

"Stargazer lilies?"

"Yes. The florist told me they're aromatic."

"That's how I knew what they were. You can put them in the vase on the kitchen counter that held the lilacs you brought me. I finally had to throw them out this morning."

"Then my timing's ideal, with these," Connor said as he ran water into the vase and inserted the flowers.

"It is." Emily picked up her coat, and Connor helped her put it on. She reached for my harness.

"Is it okay for Garth to go? Won't it be too loud for him?"

I jerked my head around to look at Emily. After the other night, I wasn't eager to let her out of my sight.

"He'll be fine. I checked with the Guide Dog Center, and they said quieter concerts—like the symphony—are fine. If we were going to heavy metal, I'd leave him home."

Relief flooded through me.

She took Connor's elbow, and we were off.

A sleek black car waited for us at the curb. A man leaned against the door, nursing a cigarette. The acrid smoke made my nostrils flare. He put it out as we approached and opened the rear door for us.

I settled on the floor between Emily and Connor. There was

plenty of room for me. I'd taken an instant dislike to the car's owner when I'd seen him smoking, but I was starting to rethink that. His backseat was roomy and comfortable.

We got out of the car at Davies Symphony Hall. I knew as soon as my paws hit the pavement that we were in for a special night. We walked under a canopy of high overhead lighting to the front doors, weaving our way through a sea of excited theatergoers. Happy conversation hung in the air. I glanced around me. We would win any award for best dressed. No contest.

"I got us tickets in the center terrace," Connor said as he handed our tickets to a woman at the door. "It's directly behind the orchestra."

"I've always wanted to sit there! That's where the chorus sits when they're performing with the symphony."

"I remember you told me that one time when you were ..." His voice trailed off.

"Trying to cajole you into going to the symphony with me?"

"Well ... yes. I'm sorry that it's taken me so long."

"It's all fine, Connor." She took his elbow and hugged it to her. "We're here now."

"Yes."

"We're starting over. Let's concentrate on having fun. If you don't enjoy the symphony, you never have to come again."

"Then again, I may discover that I love classical music."

"Tonight is the perfect opportunity to find out."

Connor led us to our seats in the middle of the row. We had to sidle past people who stood and flattened themselves against their folded seats to let us pass. Leg room here wasn't as generous as it had been in the car, but I managed to settle myself into guide dog position at Emily's feet.

The concert hall began to fill as patrons found their seats.

The buzz of conversation was interrupted by sharp bursts of sound from the orchestra.

The next thing I heard was a *tap tap tap*. The entire place fell silent. The void was soon filled with sweet tones from more than a dozen violins.

I settled my head on my paws and allowed myself to be transported. Whether Connor decided to come back or not, I hoped Emily and I would become regulars. I'd heard about patrons of the arts.

I wanted to become one.

CHAPTER 43

Connor leaned forward until he was sitting on the edge of his seat.

The strings raced to the stirring conclusion of the "Winter" concerto of Vivaldi's *Four Seasons*. The audience erupted into applause.

Emily could feel the force of Connor's clapping as his arm brushed hers. The person on her right got to his feet, still clapping. Connor followed suit. Emily stood with them. Her hands began to sting as she showed her appreciation for the performance. Bravos and applause came from all directions.

When the din began to die down, Connor bent and took her in his arms. "That was wonderful! I can't believe what I've been missing

all these years."

"You really enjoyed it?"

"Absolutely. Hearing classical music played live is much different than hearing it from a recording."

"I agree."

"Seeing the orchestra is ..." he stopped short.

"Fascinating?" Emily supplied.

"I'm sorry, Em. I didn't mean to ..."

"You can talk to me about things you see, Connor. Don't worry about hurting my feelings. You've got sight, and it's only natural to talk about what you see."

"Okay. Thank you. I've still got a lot to learn."

"You're doing just fine," Emily said, pulling back and taking Garth's harness. "I'm starved. Let's get out of here and go to dinner. What've you got planned?" She took his elbow.

"How does French cuisine sound to you?"

"Let's see—warm bread, exotic cheeses, and sauces full of butter and heavy cream. I can't think of anything better."

"I've got reservations at that new French bistro that just received a Michelin star."

"No way! How did you manage that? I'd have thought they'd be booked solid for the next year."

"I have my ways." Connor put his hand over hers as he led them through the crowd filtering out the front doors and onto the plaza. A misty rain had begun to fall. "Our car is waiting," he said, opening his jacket to hold it over her head like an umbrella and guiding her to the shelter of the backseat.

The famed restaurant was close by, and Emily and Connor were seated immediately upon their arrival. The starched white linen tablecloth almost touched the floor and provided a cozy spot for Garth to stretch out after the confines of the row of seats at the symphony.

A tuxedo-clad waiter greeted them as soon as they sat. He placed a small relish tray and a basket of warm rolls on the table.

The sommelier brought a carafe of wine and the bottle it

had come from. "As you ordered, sir," he said, holding the bottle out to Connor.

"Yes. That's it," Connor said.

The sommelier poured a taste and offered it to Connor.

"It's perfect. Thank you."

The sommelier poured a glass for Emily and set it on the table. "Your glass is at two o'clock," he said to her. He poured a glass for Connor and stepped away.

Emily sniffed her wine. "This smells wonderful." She took a sip. "Delicious."

"I took the liberty of ordering in advance," Connor said. "Since we haven't been here before, I knew you wouldn't have any favorites. I read the reviews online and picked out dishes I thought you'd enjoy. Is that all right? If you'd like to see a menu, you can still do that."

"No. This is fine."

"Do you want to know what we're going to have?"

"I don't think so. I'd like this to be a night of surprises."

"Like me discovering that I love classical music?"

Emily laughed. "I must admit, I was shocked. I figured you picked the symphony to please me—and I appreciated that—but I'm thrilled that you enjoyed it."

"I more than enjoyed it. What style is Vivaldi?"

"You mean era, I think," Emily replied. "He's considered Baroque."

The waiter brought bowls of French onion soup, its fragrant steam filling the air.

"Ohhh … I was hoping you'd ordered this." She picked up her spoon and inserted it into the gooey cheese.

"I knew we had to try this. Will you give me a crash course in classical music? I'm completely ignorant."

Emily dabbed at her lips with her napkin. "I'm no expert—

and even the experts disagree—but there are four different eras." She continued her explanation as they worked their way through cod in cider with Swiss chard, followed by a small scoop of lemon-lime sorbet and then classic duck a l'orange.

"How do you get your arms around all of it?" Connor asked.

"I think you just start listening to music. You'll learn to recognize the era, then the style and composer simply by becoming aware of their common traits."

"When I was buying our tickets for tonight, I saw that the next concert is devoted to Beethoven." He paused, then continued. "Would you like to go with me?"

Emily's smile came easily. "I'd love to."

"I'll try to get seats in the center terrace again."

"That'd be nice, but we'll be fine anywhere in the hall. Don't worry about that."

The waiter placed small plates containing sliced gruyere and chunks of brie in front of them.

"Your dessert will be out shortly."

"I don't know how I'm going to eat one more bite," Emily said. "These cheeses smell so good." She picked up her fork and speared the gruyere. "I may not make it through dessert."

"It's a pear, salted honey, and chocolate tarte tatin."

Emily moaned. "I'll have to force myself."

They finished their meal and made their way back to the waiting car for the short ride to Emily's apartment building. Once there, Connor opened Emily's door and took her hand to help her to the sidewalk. Garth stood at her side.

"Shall I wait, sir?" the driver asked.

Connor put his arms around her and drew her to him. "It's up to you," he whispered in her ear. "Can I stay?"

Emily leaned into him, inhaling the spicy scent of his after-shave. She lifted her chin, and their lips were only inches apart.

"I had a wonderful time with you tonight, Connor. It reminded me of our first date. But I ... I don't think that's a good idea."

"I understand," he said. "I can't say I'm not disappointed." He bent to kiss her as Garth sent up a high-pitched whine.

Emily stepped back quickly. "Oh my gosh—Garth. I'm sorry. I'd better take him around back to do his business," she said.

"Give me a minute," Connor said to the driver. He and Emily walked to Garth's designated spot behind the building. "I'll see you safely to your door."

When they were at her apartment, she turned to Connor and reached for him. He took her in his arms and kissed her with all the pent-up longing and desire he'd been carrying with him since he'd left for Tokyo.

Emily was the first to step back, her breathing erratic.

"What about next weekend?" Connor asked. "Will you—and Garth—come stay with me at the condo next weekend?"

"Yes," Emily said, her voice cracking with emotion. "I think we're ready."

"There's still time for me to send the driver away."

"No." Emily took a deep breath, steadying herself. "I'll see you next weekend."

CHAPTER 44

*E*mily and Garth were on their way to the trash dumpster behind the building when Garth's tail began to wag with increasing speed.

"Hey, Dhruv," Emily called.

Dhruv turned swiftly to face them. "How'd you know it was me?"

"Garth only greets one person with this much enthusiasm."

Emily wasn't able to see Dhruv flush with pleasure.

"How's your weekend going?" Emily asked.

"I went into the office for a few hours yesterday, but today I'm hanging out at home."

"I was hoping you would have gone on a date with Stephanie."

"No. I still haven't figured out where to take her."

"I don't think what you do is all that important. It's who you're with. A date is an opportunity to get to know someone better—to see if you enjoy each other's company."

"I still want it to be perfect. I'll know when I come up with the right idea." He shuffled his feet. "What've you been doing?"

"We just got up a little while ago," Emily said, covering a yawn with her hand. "We had a late night last night. I went out with Connor."

"Ahhh. Where did you go?"

"We went to the symphony and then to a fancy French restaurant for dinner."

Dhruv's head snapped up. "The symphony?"

"Yes."

"How did you like it?"

"I've always loved the symphony, but I think I enjoyed it even more now—since I've been blind. It was easier to block out everything else and focus on the music."

"That's it!"

"What do you mean?"

"The date. I'm going to ask Stephanie to the symphony."

"That's a super idea. The next program is all Beethoven pieces. I don't know when it'll be—you'll have to check online. Probably next month."

"Next month? What about the concert you just went to?"

"It closes this weekend. There might be a Sunday afternoon matinee today, but it's a bit late to ask her out."

"Why?"

"Well ... people usually make dates more than a few hours in advance. She may already have other plans."

"Then she can say no, and I'll ask her to Beethoven, later. What's wrong with that?"

"Nothing, now that you mention it. Why don't you see if there are any tickets available?"

Dhruv remained silent as he pulled up the symphony's website on his phone. "There are a handful left."

"Terrific."

They stood in silence.

"You'd better go call her, Dhruv. It's after ten, already."

"What do I say?" He sounded stricken.

"Why don't you mention that you ran into me and that I was raving about the concert Connor and I attended last night. Tell her that you know it's very last minute, but you were wondering if she'd like to go to today's matinee performance. When does it start?"

"Two."

"You'd have to pick her up by twelve thirty to get there in time."

"Saw Emily ... sorry last minute ... today's matinee," he muttered under his breath. "Got it."

Emily smiled at him. "Let me know how it goes, okay? I have a feeling that she's been anxious to hear from you."

Dhruv turned abruptly away from her and began walking. She heard him say, "Hello, Stephanie. It's Dhruv. I was wondering ..."

CHAPTER 45

$\mathcal{W}$e were in the office first thing on Monday morning. We liked to get a jump on the week. The only other person on the floor was Dhruv. He always carried a faint aroma of spicy curry, which I found delightful. We were getting Emily's first cup of coffee when Dhruv burst into the breakroom.

"It was wonderful," Dhruv said.

"She said yes?"

"Yep. The symphony was the perfect first date. We had such a wonderful time together. We talked all afternoon, and we had dinner at my favorite Mexican restaurant." The words tumbled out of him.

"Wait a minute. You can't talk at the symphony."

"No. We didn't stay there."

Emily removed her coffee cup from the brewer and brought it to her lips, blowing on the steaming liquid. "Okay—tell me all about your date."

"We went to the symphony, and it was all very nice, but we both got bored with it."

"Really?"

"Yes. At intermission, we admitted to each other that we'd fallen asleep."

"Gosh. I'm sorry to hear that. I guess my recommendation wasn't so good."

"No—it all worked out fine. We left at intermission and went to a park. We walked and talked all afternoon. We like so many of the same things. I couldn't believe it was after five when I checked my watch."

"That's a good sign—when you lose track of time."

"We went to dinner and talked some more. I finally took her home, but we could have gone on for hours."

"I'm so happy to hear this, Dhruv. It's great to find someone you can talk to so easily."

Dhruv dropped his gaze to his hands, and I could see that he was struggling with his emotions.

"I've never found it easy to talk to anyone—until Stephanie."

My heart caught in my throat, and I could see that Dhruv's statement affected Emily the same way.

"You've made my day, Dhruv. Thank you for telling me. Are you planning to see each other again?"

"This weekend," Dhruv said. "We haven't decided what to do yet, but it won't involve classical music."

CHAPTER 46

"Stephanie?" Emily answered the incoming call and settled onto the sofa. "I was just going to call you."

"Did you talk to Dhruv today?"

"First thing this morning. He caught me in the breakroom as I was getting my coffee. He was excited to tell me about your date."

"Did he say he had a good time?"

"Absolutely. Couldn't stop talking about you."

Stephanie sighed heavily. "I thought he had fun, but I wanted to make sure. It took him so long to call me for a date, I'd written him off."

"He was researching ideas for the ideal first date. He wanted everything to be perfect."

"That's what he told me."

"Did you enjoy yourself?"

"I had so much fun! The symphony wasn't our cup of tea ..."

"Sorry about that—it was my idea. Connor and I loved it."

"I'm glad you mentioned it to Dhruv. It got him to make a

178

move. I'm just glad he was flexible enough to suggest we ditch the second half and get out of there. I would never have brought it up."

"Too polite?"

"You know I am. Anyway, it was a lovely afternoon, and we walked and walked. Biscuit loved it. I think doing something active, together, allowed us both to loosen up and be comfortable with each other."

"Dhruv said you talked for hours."

"We did. We have a ton of common interests. It was all so easy. There weren't any awkward lulls in the conversation. Much better than sitting across from each other."

"Before Connor, I remember meeting new guys for coffee or a drink. Sometimes it felt like cross-examining a witness."

"Exactly. I don't know how to describe it. We just clicked."

"That's what Dhruv said." Emily felt Garth rub up against her shins. She reached down and rubbed his chest. "I'm thrilled for you. I understand you're going to see him this weekend?"

"I am. I should have said no. I'm starting my new job at the school in a month and need to find a place to live. I should be apartment hunting, but I couldn't stand not seeing him."

Emily paused, thinking. "I have an idea for you."

"What's that?"

"Why don't you and Biscuit stay in my apartment this weekend?"

"We couldn't impose on you."

"I won't be here. I'm going to spend the weekend at the condo with Connor."

"Oh, Em. I'm happy for you."

"I don't know where Connor and I are headed with our relationship, but I've got to try. Anyway, my place is already set up for accessibility and will be very convenient for apartment hunting. Plus, it'll be easy to see Dhruv."

"It would give me a taste of what it'll be like to live on my own."

"Exactly. What've you got to lose?"

"Nothing. Okay, I accept. Thank you, Emily."

"Meet me here after work on Friday. Does six o'clock work? I can give you my key, and we'll go over my setup. I'll have Connor pick me up at seven."

"Perfect. I can't wait to tell Dhruv."

"I know he'll be over the moon about this." Emily chuckled. "He'll research every available apartment in the area. You'll be in good hands."

"He's something, isn't he? Smart and funny, and so kind."

"That he is, Stephanie. Looks like two wonderful people have found each other. See you Friday."

CHAPTER 47

"*C*ome on, boy. If I don't get another cup of coffee, I'm going to be snoozing with you." Emily grasped Garth's harness. "Find Dhruv's office. Let's stop there first to see if he's heard that Stephanie will be spending the weekend at my apartment."

Dhruv was leaning toward his bank of three monitors, his hand poised over his keyboard. She heard his deep breathing.

"Good morning. We're on our way to get a cup of coffee. Want to go with us?"

"Oh, hi. Can't. I'm working on the glitch in this software update."

"I know what you're working on. I approved the request of the updates team to borrow you for this project." She paused in his doorway while he typed furiously, finally hitting the enter

button. "You're not the only one working on this issue, you know. You can take five."

"Nope. We have to find the problem."

"You've got time," Emily said, suddenly alarmed. She'd seen Dhruv work himself to the brink of exhaustion. When he had the bit between his teeth, he wouldn't stop. She heard his keyboard begin to clatter again. "Sometimes, you need to take a break and come back fresh. You'll be more productive."

"I need to fix this now. You know about Stephanie. She told me. I want to spend the weekend with her—not at the office."

"You won't need to work this weekend, even if they haven't fixed it. You're only on loan to the updates team—it's still

their responsibility."

"That's not all. I have to find it, so blind people don't get lost like you did."

Emily took a step closer to him and lowered her voice. "What

are you talking about?"

Dhruv swung his attention away from his monitors and turned to her. "This glitch in the software update caused *your* cell phone screen to freeze. Didn't you know that?"

Emily sucked in a breath. "No. I hadn't heard that. I knew there was a problem with the operating system update. The email

I received—requesting your help—said that sales were plummeting and our stock price was taking a nosedive. I know that's a massive problem. You worked in that department before you transferred to me, so I thought it made sense that they'd ask to borrow you to work on this."

"You got lost because of the problem with your phone. I was terrified when I found Garth wandering the hall of our building. I could tell he was anxious. I didn't know how we were going to find you, but I knew you were in trouble, and we had to try."

Emily's stomach did a flip-flop at the memory. "I'll admit to being terrified, at first. I did find my way to the mailbox, and I would have gotten myself home."

"I know that, Emily," Dhruv said. "Everyone isn't as resourceful as you are. I hate the idea that anyone who relies on their phone—whether they can see or not—might be in danger because the damned screen has frozen. We've got to fix this. The problem is buried somewhere in ten thousand lines of code."

She heard him swivel his chair back to his computer.

"Will you send me what you're working on? I'd like to take a crack at it." Acid pooled at the back of her throat. "If I can spare anyone what I went through, I need to try."

CHAPTER 48

Emily's feet were crossed at the ankles as she hunched forward in her chair. When she sat like this, I knew she was laser-focused on a problem. I heard Dhruv's approaching footsteps, but she didn't notice him in her doorway until he cleared his throat.

"That's it," he said. "You've found it."

"You're certain? You've double-checked my work?"

"Every bit of it. The error was really buried. I'd been through those lines of code a couple of times, and I missed it."

Emily sank against the back of her chair. "Thank goodness. I'm glad we've found the fix."

"Not 'we'—you. Come on," he said. "Time to go." My ears perked up.

"Go where?"

"There's a big meeting in the auditorium for you to present your findings."

"What're you talking about? We just found this. How can there be a meeting?"

"I let the project director know that you found the break in the code. He told his boss. His boss's boss wants everyone to get together to learn what went wrong."

"You're kidding me, right?"

"Nope. We don't want to be late. Grab your laptop."

Emily pushed her chair back from her desk, and I quickly stood up. Wherever we were going, I was ready. "But I'm not prepared."

"You don't have to be," Dhruv said. "Tell them what you found—just like you told me."

"Why are they using the auditorium?"

"So they have enough chairs." Dhruv took a step out the door. "We've got to go."

"How many people will be there?"

"I dunno. Over a hundred programmers have been working on this."

"WHAT? I hate speaking to large groups of people."

"Then pretend you're just speaking to me."

Emily tucked her laptop under her arm and pulled at my harness. I could sense the tension in her body. "Follow."

I fell in line behind Dhruv.

"Is my hair okay? Do I have lipstick on my teeth?"

"You look fine," he replied.

"You didn't even turn around and look at me, did you, Dhruv?"

I shifted my eyes from him to her. She had him dead to rights on that one. She didn't need to worry. Every hair was in place, and her teeth gleamed white.

We entered a large, windowless room that reminded me of our recent visit to the symphony. Dhruv escorted us down an aisle, flanked on either side by rows of seats that were permanently affixed to the floor. The back of the room was empty, but every seat in the first half dozen rows was filled.

We climbed a short flight of stairs that reminded me of the stair trainer at the puppy center and walked across a stage to a podium with a microphone. I stayed in position along her left side.

The audience reacted to our presence with gasps and hushed conversation.

"This is Emily Main." Dhruv spoke into the microphone, and his words were amplified into the room. "She found the error and is going to explain how she did it. She's blind, so I'm going to sync up her laptop with the Smartboard so she can use her screen reader."

The room fell silent as Dhruv got her set up. "You're all set," Dhruv said to Emily.

Emily stepped close to the microphone and engaged her screen reader. I stood at her side until I knew she had this, then sank to the floor and settled my nose on my paws, facing the audience.

I wanted to keep an eye on these people—I really tried—but the next thing I knew, they were clapping for my Emily. I stretched and got to my feet as several people from the front row made their way onto the stage and formed a line in front of Emily.

One by one, they stepped forward to shake her hand and offer a comment. I was surrounded by a sea of legs that blocked my view, but I wouldn't have been surprised to learn that everyone in the room had come up to congratulate her. I stood a little taller. My Emily was a star!

An older man who had been hanging back at the edge of the stage came forward after everyone else, except Dhruv, had left.

"That was most impressive, Ms. Main," he said. "I'm Howard Kent."

Emily's face reddened, and she held out her hand. "As in Executive Vice President of Software Engineering Howard Kent?"

I could tell that this man was important. What did they call guys like this on television—a "suit"?

The suit took her hand, and they shook. "That's me."

"Nice to meet you, sir."

"Call me Howard. Excellent presentation."

"Thank you."

"I learned a lot—and I'm not talking about programming."

Emily was silent.

He continued. "It was so interesting to see how you do your job. Your visual impairments don't hinder you in any way. You can do the same things everyone else can do. In some respects, you can do them better."

He was looking at Emily with the deep appreciation I always thought she deserved.

"It seems that way to me," Emily said. "I'm happy you agree."

He motioned for Dhruv to join them. "I owe you a debt of thanks, too," he said to Dhruv before turning back to Emily. "This guy insisted that you present your findings. He could have stepped into the limelight and taken all the credit."

"You don't know Dhruv," Emily said. "He'd never do that."

"You've both made me immensely proud of our company and our people. I'm going to put commendations in both of your personnel files, and I'm awarding you each a one-thousand-dollar discretionary bonus."

"Thank you!" they both said in unison.

"I'd better let the two of you get back to work, and I've got a plane to catch." He began to move away.

Emily took a deep breath, then called his name. "Howard—if you'd ever like to learn more about the capabilities of the visually impaired, I'd love to introduce you to my teachers at the Foundation for the Blind."

"Is that where you got your training?"

"Yes. I lost my sight a little less than two years ago. I'm still learning the technical version of braille called Nemeth."

"That's even more impressive." He paused. "I'd like to do that."

"Great."

"I'll have my assistant contact you to set something up."

"Any time."

"I'll look forward to it."

Emily, Dhruv, and I stood and waited for the suit to walk up the long aisle and exit the auditorium.

As soon as the door closed behind him, Dhruv and Emily turned to each other. Emily raised her palms above her head, and Dhruv slapped them with his. If I wasn't mistaken, this was

called high-fiving.

"A note in our files from *Howard Kent* and a thousand-dollar bonus?!" Emily cried.

"I'd say we've had a pretty good day," Dhruv said.

"What do you want to do to celebrate?" Emily asked.

"Call Stephanie and tell her," Dhruv said.

I watched Emily's perfect smile spread from ear to ear.

"You go do that," Emily said. "Now that this is all over, I'm suddenly pooped. I'm going to grab my purse, and Garth and I are going home. I think the two of us deserve an early night."

I couldn't disagree with her on that one. We hadn't gone to bed on time in a week. I needed my beauty sleep.

CHAPTER 49

"That'll be Connor," Emily said as she moved to the door. "I think we went over everything you'll need."

"I'll be fine," Stephanie called from the kitchen. "It was so nice of you to stock the fridge. You didn't have to do that."

Emily opened the door.

"Hello, gorgeous," Connor said in his native British accent that made the words seductive. He leaned in and kissed her.

Emily put her hand on his chest and lightly pushed him back. "I'd like you to meet my friend, Stephanie Wolf."

"Hello, Stephanie," Connor said.

"Nice to meet you," she replied.

"Stephanie and Biscuit are staying here while I'm gone," Emily said. "She's going to be teaching fourth grade at the elementary school nearby and looking for an apartment this weekend. I thought my place would make a convenient home base."

"Definitely," Connor said. "Good luck with all that. The rental market's tight."

"So I hear," Stephanie said. "I've made a note of every listing online, and Dhruv is going to go with me. Don't worry about me. You two get out of here and enjoy your weekend."

"My stuff is to the right of the door," Emily said.

"All of this? You used to travel light."

"Not anymore. Half of that is for Garth—his food and bowls, plus his favorite blanket and a couple of toys. I've just got a change of clothes, my laptop, and cell phone charger."

Connor grunted as he gathered everything up.

"Do you want me to take something?" Emily asked.

"No way. I've got it," Connor replied.

"What time will you be heading home on Sunday?" Emily asked Stephanie.

"Dhruv is driving me. We plan to leave at three."

"I'll be back here by two thirty to get the key."

"I can always leave it with Dhruv."

Connor shifted his load. "Why don't I take this to the car and come back for you?"

"You two get out of here," Stephanie said. "And have fun."

"Okay, Stephanie, we're off," Emily said. "Have a nice weekend. I hope you find a place. Call me if you need anything." Emily placed Garth in his harness, and they followed Connor to the elevator.

CHAPTER 50

The pizza we picked up on the way to the condo smelled amazing. Sausage and pepperoni, with green peppers and extra cheese. The aroma was like a meal in itself. Connor even placed the box on the backseat, near where I crouched on the floor. They trusted me to be a good dog and not make a lunge for it.

I *was* a very good dog. The fact that saliva was running down my jowls and puddling on the carpet below my feet was out of my control.

Emily showed me to my special spot behind the building while Connor brought our things in from the car. She unpacked my bowls and gave me fresh water and my supper before delving into hers. I was humbled by the way she put my needs first.

Connor set the pizza box on the coffee table and handed Emily a glass of wine.

She took a sip. "This is delicious."

He began rummaging in a box in the corner.

"What're you doing?"

He laid a shiny black disk on a flat circle and moved a stick-looking thing onto it. I heard an annoying crackling noise, followed by beautiful sounds like we'd heard at the symphony.

"That's Beethoven's Ninth Symphony!"

"You recognize it from the first few notes?"

"Of course I do. What have you got over there?"

"I bought a stereo-system and a collection of classical records."

"Really?"

"I read that old-fashioned vinyl is the way to go. Best sound quality."

"So, you went out and bought it?"

"One of my coworkers was selling his late father's classical record collection. It seemed like a cheap and easy way to discover what I like." He sat down on the sofa next to her. "I bought the record player online."

"You *did* enjoy the symphony the other night."

"I wasn't making that up." He put a piece of pizza on a paper plate and handed it to her before getting one for himself. "There are five cardboard boxes full of records in that corner, next to the record player. Everything else in here is right where it always was. I made sure of it. And I promise to pick up my shoes, too. I won't leave anything out for you to trip on."

She snuggled next to him and took a bite of her pizza. "Thank you, sweetheart."

"I want you to feel comfortable here. This is your home, too, Em."

They continued to eat as the music rose and fell around us. My eyelids grew heavy. At some point in the evening, they lost interest in the pizza and became more focused on each other. After an extended period of wrestling, very much like I used to do with my siblings at the puppy center, Connor picked Emily up and carried her into the bedroom.

I padded in after them, slightly offended that she hadn't thought to invite me in.

He laid her on the bed, and they resumed wrestling. They were noisier than I was with my siblings, but otherwise, it was the same. Emily had to be as tired from our long week as I was. If she wanted to play with Connor, so be it.

I found a new dog bed in the corner. It was that plush memory foam with a sheepskin cover. Very deluxe. Connor must have bought it for me. His stock was rising in my book.

I circled three times and curled up, tucking my nose under my tail. The rhythmic squeaking of the bed springs lulled me to sleep.

CHAPTER 51

*D*hruv paced in the lobby, keeping his gaze fixed on the elevator. He looked at his watch. It was still fifteen minutes before the time he and Stephanie had agreed to meet. He was going to take her apartment hunting. He didn't want her and Biscuit waiting on him.

The elevator chimed. Stephanie and Biscuit stepped out and turned toward the rear of the building.

"Hey," Dhruv called. "It's me, Stephanie."

She turned around. "Hi, Dhruv. I wanted to take Biscuit out back before we were on our way."

"Oh … of course," he said, walking with her to the grassy patch. "Do you have a list of places you want to see?"

"Yes. Five apartments. I've made a note of them on my phone." She touched her screen, and her screen reader guided her. She held it out to Dhruv. "I've got addresses and phone numbers. You can decide where we should start."

He scrolled through the list. "They're all within two miles.

This should be doable in one day. I borrowed my uncle's car, so we won't have to walk or take the bus."

"That's so nice of you. You didn't have to do that."

Dhruv shrugged. "Let's get going."

They arrived at the first apartment and were met by a landlady with a cigarette dangling from her lips.

"Your listing says that the building is smoke-free," Dhruv said.

The woman dropped her cigarette and ground it out with the toe of her shoe. "It is! I only smoke outside, in the designated area." She led them down a dimly lit hallway and opened a door at the end.

"On the first floor," the woman said, stepping aside to let them enter. "And there's a bus stop halfway down the block. Very convenient. The bedroom and bathroom are off the kitchen. I think you'll both be quite comfortable here."

"It's just for me," Stephanie said. "We're not ... I'll be the one living here."

The woman began to hack and sputter. It soon escalated into a full-throated smoker's cough. "Look around," she said, choking so hard she could barely get the words out. "Getting ... water." She turned and fled down the hall.

"What do you think?" Dhruv asked.

"It smells like an ashtray in here," Stephanie replied.

"I think so, too. Let's go on to the next place." He put her hand on his elbow, and they hurried back to his car.

The second apartment was a third-floor walkup, and the one after that was in a neighborhood that Dhruv wouldn't allow her to consider.

"Is it that bad?" Stephanie asked. "I won't be going out at night, you know."

"I wouldn't want to leave my car parked at the curb during

the daytime," he answered. "And you'll be taking Biscuit out when it's dark. It's out of the question."

"Okay," Stephanie said. "We've still got two more to look at."

When they arrived at the fourth apartment, they were told that it had just been rented.

"Darn it all," Stephanie said. "This one is closest to the school where I'll be teaching."

"The next one is only three blocks from here. Maybe we've been saving the best for last. Come on. Don't be discouraged."

They walked the short distance and pressed the buzzer for the landlord. He opened his door to them and greeted Dhruv enthusiastically. "You're here to see the apartment? It's very nice. Has big windows."

Dhruv motioned to Stephanie. Biscuit sat calmly at her side. "My friend's the one who is looking," he said.

The man took a step into the hallway, then halted. "No dogs!" he said gruffly. "We don't allow pets."

"This is a service dog," Stephanie said. "You can't refuse to rent to me *with* my dog."

The man paused, then stepped back into his apartment. "I'm sorry. I forget. The apartment's been rented. It's no longer available." He shut the door in their face.

"What the hell," Dhruv muttered. He raised his hand and pounded on the man's door.

"Forget it, Dhruv," Stephanie said, pulling his arm down.

"He can't do that. It's illegal to refuse to rent to someone because they have a Seeing Eye dog."

"I know," she said. "I just want to find an apartment. I don't want a fight."

"I'm going to report him," Dhruv said. "I'm not going to allow him to get away with this."

"Fine," Stephanie said. "I appreciate it—I do—but if that's the way he's going to treat Biscuit and me, I don't want to live in his stupid apartment."

"He's still a jerk."

"I'm tired and hungry, and I'd like to go back to Emily's."

He put her hand on his elbow. "Don't worry. We're going to find the perfect place for you."

"Maybe I should take the first one we looked at."

"No way. That wouldn't be healthy for you—or Biscuit."

"I think you're right about that."

"Let's go back to Emily's. We can order in dinner and search online for more places to look at tomorrow."

"There's nothing else in my price range." Her shoulders sagged.

"New places become available every day. I've got another neighborhood to suggest, too. It may be farther from your school, but the bus service is excellent. You'd only add five minutes to your commute."

"Thank you, Dhruv. You're always looking for a solution, aren't you?"

Dhruv walked taller as he guided her back to the car. "That's what I do," he said. "Look for solutions."

***

By the time they'd worked their way through two racks of barbeque ribs, jalapeno corn bread, shoestring potatoes, and a mountain of coleslaw, they'd selected six more apartments to view the next day.

"Thank you, Dhruv," Stephanie said. "I was so discouraged, but I'm feeling much better now."

"If none of these work out," he said, tapping her phone with his finger, "we'll keep looking. You'll find somewhere great."

"Emily said that you're the most persistent person she's ever known," Stephanie said. "I'm sorry that I'm taking up your entire weekend. Don't you have anything planned?"

"I do have plans for tonight," he said.

She snapped back in her chair. "I'm sorry—I guess I should let you go."

"They involve you," he said. "Would you like to come to my apartment?"

"Oh … um … all right."

"I have a surprise for you. I think you'll like it." He rose from Emily's kitchen table and gathered up the empty to-go containers. "Get Biscuit. I'll put this in the dumpster while you take him out. Then we can get started."

Stephanie hesitated, then rose slowly to her feet. Going to his apartment probably didn't mean what such a suggestion would have meant when she was a college girl. A smile played on her lips. Not that she would mind.

As they headed to his apartment, her curiosity got the better of her. "So … what's this big surprise?"

"Dominoes," he said. "You said that you and your family used to love to play dominoes. And that you miss it."

Stephanie laughed. "I can't believe you remembered that."

"I found accessible ones online. They're white with black raised dots the size of a pea. The dots aren't braille—they're the regular domino dots. I got dark green felt to cover my dining room table, and I've put a bright task light next to it. We can play a version called Chicken Foot. It's like the card game Old Maid."

"Dhruv," Stephanie said, blinking hard. "This is incredibly thoughtful of you. I can't get over how nice you are."

He guided her to the table and held out a chair for her.

"I have to warn you; I'm good at dominoes. I'm not going to let you win, just because you're blind."

Stephanie laughed as she reached out and examined a domino. "You won't have to. I plan to beat you fair and square."

After playing four games, to a tie at two games each, Stephanie folded her hands in front of her on the table. "I'm bushed," she said. "I've got to get some sleep."

"Okay." Dhruv got to his feet. "I'll walk you to your door."

They escorted Biscuit to the grassy patch on the way.

Dhruv took her hand, and they stood in silence.

He continued to hold her hand as they made their way into the elevator and down the hall, dropping it only when she had to fish in her purse for the key.

She unlocked the door and turned back to him.

"What a wonderful day, Dhruv. I had such a great time with you."

"Me too," he said. He didn't turn to walk away. "I have a question," he finally said.

"What's that?"

"Will you play a tie-breaker game with me?"

Stephanie laughed and stood on her tiptoes, brushing a light kiss on his lips. "Of course I will. Anytime. Goodnight, Dhruv," she said before stepping inside and closing the door.

Dhruv stood in place long after the deadbolt clicked shut. When he finally turned away and headed to his apartment, his smile

radiated his happiness.

CHAPTER 52

*E*mily woke on her side, Connor's arm across her body. She sank back against his body, and he tightened his arm, holding her close.

He kissed the back of her head and moved to her ear.

She patted his arm before wriggling out of his embrace. "I need to take Garth out."

Connor turned over and looked at the bedside clock. "It's almost nine."

"We didn't get to sleep until after two," she replied, putting on the dress slacks that lay on the floor in the pile of her hastily discarded clothing. She drew on her sweater and put Garth into his harness.

"What would you like to do today?" Connor asked.

"I haven't thought about it."

"I've got an idea. Want me to tell you about it?"

"Nope," she said as she and Garth headed for the door. "Surprise me."

"I've got croissants from our favorite bakery. And fresh-squeezed juice," he called after her.

"Wonderful!" The door closed behind her.

***

"I can smell the Pacific," Emily said. "We're close, aren't we?"

"I'm impressed. We're in the Presidio."

"The sun is warm on my face. It's a perfect day for a walk."

"We're not going for a walk. We'll be doing a lot of walking, but we'll be inside."

"Now I'm intrigued."

"We always talked about going here but never found the time," Connor said, turning to her.

"The Walt Disney Family Museum?"

"Yep. I went online and learned that they have an audio-described tour for the visually impaired. I figured we'd check it out."

"Brilliant idea!"

"We can stay as long as you like. The minute you want to leave, just let me know. Even if it's only ten minutes."

Emily laughed. "You won't be able to get me out of there in ten minutes. I was besotted with Disney princesses when I was little."

"Now, why doesn't that surprise me?"

"Let's get this show on the road," Emily said.

Connor led them to the ticket counter and then into the museum.

Garth behaved in top-of-class guide dog fashion.

The museum became crowded on this Saturday morning, and by noon, Emily switched off her headphones and leaned into Connor. "I'm ready to go whenever you are."

"All right, then."

"We don't have to rocket out of here. Whenever you're ready."

"There's so much; you can't see it all in one visit. We can come back another time."

"That would be fun. I've thoroughly enjoyed this," Emily said as the three of them made their way out of the exhibit.

"There's a restaurant here. We can get lunch and take it out to the lawn to eat if you want."

"I'd love that." She stopped suddenly. "There's one more thing. Can we stop at the gift shop on the way out?"

Connor chuckled. "Do you want me to buy you a Disney princess doll?"

Emily cuffed his arm. "It's not for me, silly. I'd like to find a little gift for Zoe."

"The sign says the gift shop is down this hallway. What do you want to get her?"

"Definitely not a stuffed animal," Emily said. "Sabrina will think it's a dog toy. Maybe a piece of jewelry? There should be a section with costume jewelry."

"We're here," Connor said. "This place is packed. I think I see a display in the corner that might be what you want."

He put her hand on his elbow, and the other shoppers politely allowed them to pass by. A child yelled, "Doggy!" A woman replied that the doggy was working and they couldn't pet him.

"Bravo to her," Emily said.

Connor stopped.

"What've we got?"

"We're standing next to a display of four glass shelves. There's jewelry on all four sides."

"What's the color of the metal, and what kinds of pieces are they?"

"Mostly silver. There are rings, necklaces, and bracelets. There're also some hair thingies."

Emily pursed her lips. "Do you know what a charm bracelet is?"

"My mother used to wear one. I was fascinated by it as a kid." He led them to the other side of the display. "There's a whole bunch of them over here."

"I got one for Christmas when I was Zoe's age and had so much fun collecting charms. I'll bet she'd love it. What do they look like?"

Connor scrutinized the display of charm bracelets. "They have two different kinds. One has flat charms that are painted to look like a princess. There are other flat, painted charms that I'm assuming are objects from her story."

"Are they pretty?"

Connor hesitated. "I'm no connoisseur of little girl's jewelry, but I think they look pretty tacky. The other style of bracelet is much better. More like the one I remember my mom having."

"Can you describe it to me?"

"Each princess has her own bracelet. All the charms are three-dimensional silver, and there are faceted, colorful stones between each silver charm."

"That sounds nice."

"Much better, in my opinion." He found a price tag. "They're twice as expensive as the other style."

"I don't care about that." Emily paused. "I think Zoe's favorite Disney princess is Belle—from *Beauty and the Beast*."

Connor rummaged through the bracelets hanging from a Lucite bar, sending up a clatter of tinkling metal.

"Do they have a bracelet for her?"

"Just a sec. I have no idea who Belle is, so I have to look at every tag, and they're all tangled up."

"She wears a big yellow dress. There are probably also charms of a teapot, a candelabra, and a wardrobe."

"Got it!" He fished the bracelet out from the end of the row. "It's the only one of hers."

"Are you sure?"

"That's what it says on the tag." He placed it in her hand.

Emily felt the charms. "This must be it! I can't wait to give it to her."

She purchased the bracelet and they backtracked to the restaurant.

"It sounds like there's a lot of people in there," Emily said.

"It's pretty busy. Would you like to go somewhere else?"

"No. Can you go in without us and get our food? You know what I like."

"Of course. Hang tight and I'll be right back."

Garth and Emily waited in the hallway while Connor purchased tuna salad sandwiches, chips, and large sodas. He escorted them out of the museum and found a spot on a bench by the green lawn that overlooked the bay.

They sank against the wooden slats of the bench and relaxed in the sunshine, chatting about their morning in the museum.

"The long wall of Mickey Mouse drawings that were used to produce fifteen seconds of Steamboat Willie was astounding to me. They were drawn by hand," Connor said.

"It's hard to get your head around. All of that's done by computer now." Emily turned her face over her shoulder. "Clouds are coming in, aren't they?"

A gust of wind caught her jacket and sent the wrapping from their sandwiches flying.

Connor chased them down. "They predicted heavy rain this evening. Looks like it's moving in now. Ready to go?"

Emily stood. "Yep. I've had a blast. Thank you for planning this."

"What would you like to do for the rest of the day?"

"That wind has a bite in it. Why don't we head back to the condo? We can unpack your new record collection and order in dinner."

"I'd love that," he said. "I'm anxious to see what I bought, and you'll know how to organize everything. You're much better at that than I am."

"Do you have someplace to put them?"

"I bought special shelves. They're in boxes along the wall. I have to put them together."

"Sounds like we've got a project. Let's go."

"You don't mind?"

"I'm happy to help you, Connor. It's your turn."

CHAPTER 53

$\mathcal{I}$ sensed that the day was not getting off to a good start when Emily and I stepped back into the condo after she'd taken me out for my morning walk. Connor was in the kitchen, opening and shutting cabinet doors in rapid succession and slamming drawers. I don't consider myself a connoisseur, but I was certain he'd let the butter burn before he fried their eggs.

Emily moved to the counter and found the Ziplock bag with my kibble. She scooped the right amount into my bowl and put it on the floor for me. "What's wrong?"

"We're out of coffee," he grumbled. "I can't believe I forgot it at the store."

"No worries," Emily said. "Garth and I can go to the coffee shop on the next block to pick it up while you finish …"

"Burning eggs?" Connor cut her off. "I'll go. I've got to chuck these," he said, rattling a pan on the burner. "I'll make new ones when I get back."

"Don't be silly. We can be there and back by the time you finish making breakfast."

"I'm not sending my blind wife out to run an errand because I'm a bloody idiot."

"Your blind wife," Emily emphasized the words, "is more than capable of running errands."

"What if you get turned around—what if you get lost?" Connor tipped the pan, and the inedible eggs slipped into the sink, where they landed with a splat.

"I've got Garth and my cane with me. Even if I didn't, I could find my way home. They taught us techniques at the foundation."

"Really? I hate to break this to you, but things you learn in a classroom don't always work in real life."

I could see the back of Emily's neck get red.

"As a matter of fact, I've used these techniques—in a real-life situation."

Connor let the pan clatter onto the countertop and swung to face her. "What're you talking about?"

Emily took a deep breath and straightened. "I tried to go to a restaurant near my apartment the other night and got lost. I encountered an obstruction—a portion of the sidewalk was under construction—and got turned around."

"Didn't Garth lead you around it?"

"I left him at home."

"What? Why on earth did you do that?"

"We're supposed to go out on our own. We need to keep our cane skills sharp, and our dogs need to learn how to stay home alone."

"Why didn't you call me?"

"My touch screen froze."

"Oh, Em. That must have been terrifying!" He crossed to where she was standing and took her into his arms.

"I have to admit I was scared."

"I'll bet you were. We won't let that happen again."

"How do you propose to do that?"

"I'll be with you when you go out. If you need something, you can order it and have it delivered. You never have to be out on your own."

I watched Emily's spine stiffen. She stepped back from him. He was treading on thin ice.

"That would make me a prisoner in my own home, Connor! I don't want that. I need to live my life as an independent adult. That's the point of everything I learned at the foundation—it's why I have Garth."

"And look how much good all of that did you." He slapped the counter with his open palm. "You still got lost, didn't you?"

"You're not listening to me!" Emily was now yelling. "I got lost, but I *also found my way home*. Without Garth and without my phone! I'm very proud of that."

"Okay," he said, rubbing his hand across the stubble on his chin. "I can understand that. How did you do it?"

Emily told him about retracing her steps to the sidewalk obstruction and then finding her way to the mailbox.

"That's impressive," he said. "I'm proud of you, too."

"Thanks."

"I still think it's better not to get lost in the first place."

Emily sighed in exasperation. "Of course it is, but even sighted people get lost at times."

"That's true, but it's easier for us to find our way. That settles it—you'll be safer living here, with me."

"So you can hover over me?"

"That's not what I meant."

"You're smothering me, Connor."

"And you're not dealing with the reality of your situation. I need to watch over you."

They faced each other, both of them breathing hard.

"I can't be happy living like that."

"I'm sorry, Em. I don't want you to be unhappy. I … I just don't know what to do to help."

I sidled up to Connor and rubbed against him. I could see that he needed moral support.

Emily stepped toward Connor and put her hand on his arm. "I know. We're both still learning how to live with my blindness."

"What do you want to do now?"

"Garth and I are going to get coffee while you make us eggs and toast." She leaned in and kissed him lightly. "And you're not going to worry about us."

"I can't promise that, but I'll try. What about after breakfast? It's almost eleven now."

"We'll have an hour before we have to leave to take me home." She kissed him again. "We can think of something."

He held her tight. "And next weekend? Shall we give it another go?"

Emily relaxed in his arms.

I thumped my tail on the floor.

"Definitely. I think we should."

CHAPTER 54

*C*onnor rolled over the following Saturday morning and extended his arm to the other side of the bed. The covers were thrown back, but the spot where Emily had been sleeping was still warm. He propped himself on an elbow and heard her voice from the living room.

Garth lay curled up on his bed in the corner, but his ears were alert. He, too, was listening.

Connor couldn't make out her words, but her tone contained an urgency and a touch of alarm. He got out of bed and padded to the doorway.

"I'll go straight to the hospital," she said into her phone, "and I'll call you when I'm done." She tapped the screen to end the call.

"Martha?" Connor asked.

Emily spun to him, clutching her chest. "You scared me. I didn't know you were awake."

"I'm sorry. I gather something's happened to Zoe's grandmother."

"That's just it—they don't know. She's still in the rehabilitation hospital and is making progress. They're telling her it'll take time and to be patient."

"That sounds promising."

"I know, but Mom visited her yesterday, and Irene told her that she feels like something is very wrong with her. They just can't seem to find it."

"I very much doubt that," he said.

"Mom said the same thing to her, but there was no reassuring her."

"That must be frustrating for Martha. No wonder she called you."

"It's not just that. Irene wants to see me—today. She told Mom that she has something important to discuss with me."

"Why don't you call Irene?"

"Mom suggested that to her, but she insisted that she wants to talk to me in person. Mom said that she was almost frantic about it."

"Sounds like we now have plans for our Saturday. We're going to the hospital so you can see Irene."

"That won't be much fun for you. I can take a rideshare. I'll see Irene, and then I'll want to go by Mom's to check on Zoe. I can be home for dinner."

"Nonsense. I'm taking you. End of discussion. Do I have time for a quick shower before we leave?"

"Yes. I'll tend to Garth and then pull myself together. Can we leave in half an hour?"

"Absolutely." He took a step toward the bathroom, then turned back and took her in his arms. "Try not to worry, Em. She's well cared for. Everything's going to be fine."

"Her intuition about herself ... unnerves me. Irene strikes me as a very no-nonsense woman."

"What is it you told me your grandmother always said? Don't borrow trouble? We'll know soon enough. Don't let your imagination run away with you."

"Thanks, Connor." She kissed his cheek and gave him a playful shove towards the bathroom.

"Let's stop at your place on the way to grab that bracelet you bought for Zoe at the museum."

"Genius idea," she called before she and Garth headed to his spot outside.

CHAPTER 55

*E*mily moved her hand from the hospital bed's railing to
the unyielding mattress and gingerly felt for Irene's
arm. The nurse had assured her that Irene knew that Emily was
coming—had been excited about the visit—but had fallen
asleep.

Emily put her hand into the older woman's. She wouldn't
wake her—at least not yet. Emily stood at the bedside, listening
to Irene's rhythmic breathing.

Garth lay at her feet, his hindquarters under the bed and his
nose pointing out.

A cart clattered noisily in the hallway. Irene startled, jerking
her hand out of Emily's. She opened her eyes, and it took
her a moment to focus.

"Emily," she said. "I didn't hear you come in. How long have
you been here?"

"Not long."

"My gosh." She pressed a button on her side rail and raised
the head of her bed. "Thank you for coming, dear."

"Of course," Emily replied. "Mom said that you wanted to see me." She started to withdraw her hand, but Irene reached out and grasped it with both of hers.

"I'm not well," she said. "I'm afraid I'm not going to get out of here."

"Mom said your recovery is slower than expected, but that they're telling you this happens and to be patient. You'll still recover and be able to go back home again."

"That's what they're saying." She sighed heavily and pulled Emily's hand to her chest. "I know my body, Emily. I know something's wrong—even if they can't find it. I want to get better—I'm praying I get better—but I don't think I will."

"It's natural to worry, but ..."

Irene cut her off. "I'm not afraid of dying. I believe in an afterlife. I'm anxious to see my dear husband—I miss Alfred every day. And my daughter—Zoe's mother. What I'm worried about—who I'm fighting to stay alive for—is Zoe."

Emily felt Irene's hand tremble.

"That little girl has been through so much, what with losing both of her parents in that car accident. I can't bear the thought of her going into foster care."

"It's not going to come to that."

Irene's voice rose. "Maybe not, but I need to make arrangements for her—just in case something happens to me."

"What about her other grandparents?"

"They're both deceased. Her dad was an only child. She has no one but me." Irene's voice cracked on the words that followed. "And you."

Emily stood in silence.

"I'm asking you, Emily—no, *begging* you. Will you be Zoe's legal guardian if something happens to me?" She continued in a rush. "I know it's a tremendous thing to ask, but I think you love Zoe. She certainly loves you."

Emily leaned over the bed, bringing her face close to Irene's.

Garth got to his feet and rested his head on Emily's thigh.

"I'm leaving my estate to Zoe. I'm not rich, but there'll be plenty of money to support her. And put her through college. She won't be an economic burden on you."

"Don't worry about that." Emily managed to force out the words. "I'm … overcome … that you would trust me with her. I love Zoe with all my heart and would be honored to serve as her guardian. I hope that it never becomes necessary. I don't think it will."

"I can count on you?"

Emily felt tears drip onto their joined hands. She didn't know if they were hers or Irene's. "You … can … count … on … me."

Irene drew in a ragged breath. "Thank you, dear. This gives me such comfort. I've already spoken to my lawyer. I'll have her draw up the necessary paperwork."

"I'm sure we'll never need it."

"I'm working as hard as I can to get better," Irene said, letting her hand fall to her side. "I don't want to die. But this puts my mind at ease. You have no idea."

"I'm glad." Emily patted her hand.

"Thank you for coming all the way out here, on your Saturday," Irene said.

"I was glad to do it. I'm going to check on Zoe now, before I head back to the city."

"You won't say anything about this, will you? I'd like to tell her if—and when—the time comes."

"No. I agree that there's no point in upsetting Zoe about something that I don't think will ever happen."

"You're a wise young woman, Emily. I'll be at peace if I have to leave her."

They both turned at a knock on the door. A young man stood there, holding a walker. "Time for your physical therapy, Ms. Irene. Let's do one more lap around the nurse's station than we did this morning."

"I'm always up for a walk with a handsome young man," Irene said. "And you," she said to Emily, "had better be on your way. I know my granddaughter will be most anxious to see you."

Emily laughed. "I'm sure she will. You can have your attorney contact me if she needs anything from me. I'll clear out of your way."

"Thank you again, Emily."

"My prayers are with you, Irene. For your full recovery." Emily picked up Garth's harness, and they headed to the waiting room at the end of the unit.

Connor tossed the old issue of *Sports Illustrated* that he'd been half-heartedly thumbing through onto an institutional chrome-and-glass end table.

"How is she? How'd it go?"

Emily bit her lip.

"You look upset."

"No." She inhaled deeply. "She's struggling. I think she'll get better."

"Do you want to talk about it?"

"Not now—I just can't. Let's get to Mom's. Maybe we can take her and Zoe out for a late lunch."

"Whatever you want," Connor said, placing her hand on his elbow and leading them to his car.

CHAPTER 56

J got to my feet and pressed my nose against the glass of the passenger-side rear window. I recognized the neat bungalow. I knew we'd be greeted by tantalizing aromas from the kitchen. If we were lucky, we might even smell one of my favorites: freshly baked apple pie. We were at Mom's.

Before Emily and I reached the steps to the front porch, the door flew open and banged against the large pot of red geraniums next to it. Zoe erupted from inside and raced toward us.

"Emily!" she cried, plowing into her and throwing her arms around Emily's waist.

"Hello, Zoe." Emily pulled the girl to her and held her close.

I sat down and let the two of them enjoy the moment.

"Can I say hi to Garth? He's in his harness, so I know he's working, but ..."

"It's all right." Emily bent to me. "It's okay, boy."

Zoe dropped to her knees and showered me with affection.

I tried to maintain a sense of decorum but soon found myself on my back, wriggling and reaching out with my tongue to swipe

at Zoe's face.

Martha came out to join us.

"How'd it go?" she asked quietly.

Emily shook her head almost imperceptibly. "I'll tell you later."

Connor clasped his hands and rubbed them together.

"Anybody hungry?"

"I am!" Zoe shot to her feet.

"Why don't I take all of you to lunch? It's not often that I get to dine with three such lovely ladies."

"I'm in the midst of putting together an apple pie for the church bake sale tomorrow," Martha said. "You all go on without me."

"Then it's down to you, Zoe. What would you like to eat?"

"I want a hamburger and a chocolate shake."

"Exactly what I was thinking about," he said. "And I know just where to take us. Can we bring something back for you?" he called to Martha.

"I'm good, thank you."

Zoe climbed into the backseat with me, tucking her feet carefully to one side. "Don't worry, Garth. I'm not going to kick you."

I licked her knee. I knew she'd never intentionally do anything

to hurt me.

We arrived at the restaurant as the lunch crowd was thinning out. We were shown to our table without having to wait. The waitress handed each of them a stiff, plastic-coated menu. I lifted my nose in the air. Fried fish was being served, along with french fries and chicken, but the odor of grilled hamburger floated above all the others. Zoe would be happy. I approved.

A waiter placed small paper napkins in front of each of them with the precision of someone dealing cards from a deck. He set a glass on each napkin and poured water from a pitcher without spilling a drop. "What'll it be?" he asked.

They placed their orders.

Zoe leaned across the table to Emily. "How come you're here?"

Emily paused, considering whether she should say that they'd come to visit Irene. The knowledge would only upset Zoe.

"Emily's got a present for you," Connor said.

The little girl began to bounce in her chair. "Really?"

"Yes," Emily said, shooting a smile in Connor's direction. "We went to the Walt Disney Family Museum last weekend. I got it for you in the gift shop."

"I'll get to go there in sixth grade," Zoe said. "It's one of the sixth-grade field trips. I can't wait."

The waitress placed a large chocolate shake on the table in front of Zoe, followed by sodas for Connor and Emily.

"Wow," Zoe said. "This thing is huge."

"There's even more in this silver cup," he said, tapping a tall, frosty cylinder with his spoon. "They couldn't fit it all in your glass."

Zoe wrapped her lips around the straw and sucked down a large gulp.

"Don't feel like you have to finish it," Connor said.

"Are you kidding? I want all of this."

Connor chuckled. "You're determined."

Emily put a small box, wrapped in white paper with a red bow, on the table and pushed it toward Zoe.

"Here. I had one of these when I was your age, and I loved it. I thought you might find it cool, too."

Zoe tore off the wrapping. "Ohhhh," she cried as she opened the box. She lifted the charm bracelet from the pillow of cotton fluff that surrounded it. "This is so pretty!"

"It's a charm bracelet," Emily said.

Zoe turned it around in her hand, examining all the charms. "It's *Beauty and the Beast*! My favorite."

Emily beamed. "I thought I remembered that."

"I like it that Belle's a bookworm. Like me."

"Do you want me to help you put it on?" Connor asked.

"Yes. Which hand do I put it on?"

"You're right-handed, so you'd wear it on your left."

Zoe stuck her left hand out to Connor, and he fastened the clasp. She raised her hand in the air and shook it, delighting in the tinkle of the charms.

The waitress brought their food. "I see somebody's got a beautiful charm bracelet," she said, placing a plate in front of Zoe.

"I just got it! You wanna see?" Zoe thrust her hand out to the woman.

"This is so pretty. Very grown-up. I'd like to have a bracelet like that myself."

Zoe flushed with pride. "I can't wait to show Gramma. If she's better, we're going to see her tomorrow."

Emily froze, her hamburger halfway to her mouth. She replaced it on her plate and took a sip of her soda instead.

Connor searched Emily's face. He cleared his throat. "I'm glad you like to read," he said. "Tell me about your favorite book."

Zoe chewed and swallowed. "I've just started reading Nancy

Drew. She's a detective. There's a whole bunch of books in her series."

Zoe swung her feet under the table. I lay down, positioning myself out of their path.

Emily relaxed as Zoe picked up steam on the subject of the famous girl detective.

CHAPTER 57

"Call me tomorrow night," Emily whispered in her mother's ear as they hugged goodbye in the driveway. "After Zoe goes to bed."

"Okay, honey. Thanks for coming out. I'm sure Irene appreciated it," she said softly, "and Zoe and I loved seeing you."

"Bye, Zoe," Connor said. "Maybe we can plan a trip to the museum next time."

"That'd be so neat!" Zoe said. "I don't want to wait until I'm in sixth grade."

"We'd better get going," Emily said. She opened the door to the backseat, and Garth hopped into place. She and Zoe hugged.

"Thank you, again, for my bracelet," Zoe said.

"You're welcome. You call me anytime, you understand. I'm always here for you."

"Okay, Emily." Zoe's voice was small.

Emily got into the car, and Connor backed out of the driveway.

"You were just wonderful with her, Connor. I'll bet she's going to have a big ole crush on you."

"She's a very sweet little girl," he said. "I'm not good with children—no experience, really—but we seem to get along."

"You do. I appreciate that you made an effort with her."

"I could tell that you were still upset by your visit with Irene."

They sat in silence.

"Martha was right. She's not doing well, is she?"

"That's just it." Emily swiveled to him. "They keep telling her she'll be fine, but she has a deep sense that she won't be."

"Wouldn't her doctors know best?"

"Not necessarily. I'm a big believer in knowing your own body."

He reached over and took her hand. "That must be upsetting. I don't know what she expected you to do about it."

"She didn't ask me to come see her to discuss her care." Emily inhaled slowly. "Irene wanted to make plans—for Zoe—in
case she dies."

"What does that have to do with you? I bet it's tough for her to think about, but doesn't Zoe have other family?"

"She doesn't. Zoe would go into the foster care system."

"That'd be rough."

"Exactly. I'm so glad you understand that."

He took his eyes off the road and looked at her. "What do you mean?"

"She asked if I would agree to become Zoe's legal guardian
if she dies."

"Whoa. That's a colossal responsibility. It's like you become a parent."

Emily remained silent.

"We'd need to think about that. Taking on Zoe's care would radically change our lives."

"I said yes," Emily said quietly. "I told Irene that I love Zoe and would serve as her guardian. Without reservation."

Connor jerked back into his seat. "WHAT?"

"You heard me. I agreed to become her guardian." She raced on. "Irene's leaving all of her assets to Zoe. She wouldn't be a financial burden."

"To hell with the money. I'm not concerned about that. We'd become parents! We talked about this at length before we got married. Neither one of us wanted kids. We were always in agreement on that score."

"I know that."

"It'll change everything we do. Zoe will be a factor in our every decision." He fired his words in rapid succession. "We haven't adjusted to your being blind yet. Hell … we haven't even figured out how to make our marriage work."

"I love Zoe, Connor. I couldn't stand by and allow her to go into the system. You know that's a horrible option. What did you expect me to do?"

"Talk to me about it first," he said. "At least give me the courtesy of asking for my input."

"I see." She was seething. "Like you asked me before you took the job in Tokyo."

He gripped the steering wheel tightly.

"They're not the same thing."

"Oh, no? You decided to make a big life decision—to move to the other side of the world—before I'd even learned how to walk down the block."

"Having a child to care for is a major disruption to our lives."

"Like pulling me away from my training center, my mom,

and my job wouldn't be a major disruption."

"Well ... now we're even, aren't we?"

"Is that how it is?" Emily asked.

"Look—I was wrong when I made the decision to take the Tokyo job without your input. We've gone over this. Mea culpa! I thought we were going to do better in the future."

Emily put her palms on her temples. "I'm sorry. I should have talked to you first. Irene was so earnest—so desperate to have closure on this issue. I was caught up in her anxiety. Can you understand that?"

Connor drummed his thumbs on the steering wheel, thinking. "I guess so."

"We're probably arguing over nothing. The doctors say she'll be fine. In fact, she perked up when the physical therapist came to work with her. Maybe knowing that she doesn't have to worry about Zoe—if the worst happens—will help her get better." She rested her hand on the console between them. He put his hand on top of hers.

"I thought that you were having fun with Zoe today."

"I was. She's great." He moved his hand away from hers. "That doesn't mean I want to be a parent—either to my own child or to Zoe."

Emily swallowed hard. "What do you want for your life, Connor? Where do you see yourself ... in five years? Ten?"

"I loved working in Tokyo, but I acknowledge that the timing was wrong. I should never have taken that job while you were adjusting to your vision loss."

"Go on."

"I'd still like to live and work internationally. Together—with you. You've shown me that all of those things are still possible for you. I realize our dream may have been delayed, but it doesn't have to be derailed." He glanced over at her. "Do you think you can lead your life in another country?"

"I'm sure I can," she said quietly. "It's just that I don't want to, anymore."

They sat in silence as the miles slid by.

When they crossed the bridge into the city, Emily turned to him. "This has been an emotional day. I'm exhausted."

"Me, too."

"How about we take a break for the rest of the weekend. I need to study my braille, and you said that you have a proposal to work on tomorrow afternoon."

He shrugged. "If that's what you want."

"We're both out-of-sorts. Let's give each other the chance to think about things."

"I suppose you're right. Shall we try this again next weekend?"

"I'd like that," Emily said. "I want you to be happy, Connor. I want us both to be happy."

CHAPTER 58

J opened my eyes when I heard the familiar ping indicating that Emily had logged off her computer. The sun behind the Venetian blinds in our office was a bit brighter than it usually was when she left for the day. Maybe we were going home early. I'd guided Emily to the break room for coffee three times since lunch. She was tired from our emotional weekend with Irene and the subsequent fight with Connor. So was I.

Her phone announced an incoming text. Emily hovered over

the message from Gina: "I've got big news. Can we talk?"

Emily dictated her response. "Like how big?"

"BIG."

"As in the bar at the Four Seasons big?"

"Yes!"

"Meet you there in thirty minutes?" Emily replied.

"On my way. You're the best," came Gina's response.

Emily hastily gathered our gear. "We're going to a very fancy hotel, Garth," she told me as she slipped my working harness over my head. "You'll need to be on your best behavior."

I gave an indignant shake. When was I ever not on my best behavior?

"Gina and I meet at the Four Seasons to toast every major milestone," she said as we made our way to the elevator. "Like when she got into UCLA, and I got this job." We stepped into the elevator. "And when I got engaged to Connor."

I put my shoulders back. I didn't know how far we'd have to walk to get to this Four Seasons place, but I was ready for my mission.

We exited the building where we worked, and Emily stopped abruptly. "We're calling a rideshare," she told me. "I want to get there first and secure a table by the window. The views of downtown from the fifth floor are spectacular. Gina's always loved them."

We were getting a ride? I could do that.

Twenty minutes later, we were being shown to a table by the window. I perused the view before settling into my spot at Emily's feet. She hadn't exaggerated—the city was breathtaking from this vantage point.

"A bottle of Veuve Clicquot, please," Emily told the waiter. "And two glasses."

"Are you celebrating something special?"

"Yes." Emily illuminated him with her smile. "I don't know what, yet. I'll find out when my friend gets here."

"Very good, madam. I'll bring it right out."

"Thank you." Emily reached across the table and found a trifold card. She scrolled to the app on her phone that recognized print and used it to read the appetizer menu.

The waiter brought the champagne and uncorked it, pouring her a glass.

The sweet, fizzy liquid had pungent undertones.

"Will you also put in an order for the blistered shishito peppers and the cheese board?"

"Great choices. Who are you waiting for?"

"Her name is Gina."

"I'll ask the host to bring her over as soon as she arrives."

"Thank you."

I knew she would be here any minute. I recognized incoming Chanel No. 5.

She saw us sitting by the window and made her way directly to us.

"Em," she called as she came to our table. "You're early."

"I wanted to snag a table with a view," she said. "I know how much you love it."

Gina leaned over Emily, and the two women hugged in the awkward way people do when one is standing and the other is sitting. I'd always thought dogs were much better at greeting each other than people are. We go all in, getting down on the floor and rolling around with each other. There's no doubt in anyone's mind when two dogs are excited to see each other.

Gina slipped into the chair across from Emily. "And Veuve!"

"You said it was big news," Emily said, leaning across the table. "Don't keep me in suspense any longer."

Gina took a deep breath. "I'm engaged!"

"Oh, Gina! I hoped that would be it. Congratulations! I'm so happy for you."

"Thank you."

"Do you have a ring?"

"He wants me to pick it out. We're going shopping on Saturday."

"That's so fun! I'm glad you can get exactly what you want. You'll have to show it to me the minute you get it."

Gina was silent.

"I've still got a pinhole of vision in my left eye. I intend to hover over your left hand to get a good look at it."

The waiter put their appetizers on the table between them and poured a glass of champagne for Gina.

Emily picked up her glass. "To Gina and Craig. May my best friend have the happy marriage she so richly deserves."

They clinked glasses, and both of them took a sip of the amber liquid.

"Do you mean that, Em?"

"That I want you to have a happy marriage? Of course I do."

"Not that. What you said—about my being your best friend." Her voice cracked on the final two words.

Emily extended her left hand, palm up.

Gina placed her hand into Emily's.

"Of course I mean it, Gina."

"You forgive me?"

"I don't think there's anything to forgive." Emily squeezed her hand before letting it go. "I want to focus on the future."

"Will you help me plan my wedding?"

"Duh. You told me your mom and dad are still on their retirement world tour. Who else is going to do it?"

Gina laughed. "Not Craig. He said the only thing he wants a say in is what he wears. He's specified either a black tuxedo or a blue suit."

"You mean he won't consider a kilt?"

Gina laughed. "I know. He's such a spoilsport."

"Seriously. What are you thinking?"

Gina poured them each another glass of champagne. They began to snack on the appetizers. Their waiter zoomed by as the restaurant started to fill up.

"I'd like to get married at the inn that Craig took me to. We could have a ceremony on the cliffs, overlooking the ocean."

"At sunset?"

"Exactly."

"Lovely."

They leaned toward each other.

"The reception could be in their walled garden. There's a built-in bar and plenty of room for tables and a dance floor."

Their words came faster and faster. They were soon talking over each other, finishing each other's sentences. I wasn't too sure what they were saying, but my ears perked up when I heard my name mentioned. Gina was suggesting I wear a vest and bowtie that would match Emily's dress. Emily was going to be a matron of honor—whatever that is. I knew both of their hearts were happy.

I rested my face on my paws. We were going to be here for a while. I allowed my eyes to close. My Emily was enjoying herself. I was in no hurry to go anywhere.

CHAPTER 59

"That's a lot of money for that tiny apartment," Stephanie said as she and Biscuit got back into the car.

"It's definitely overpriced," Dhruv said. "Any more on your list?"

"That's the last one." She exhaled and shook her head. "I think I'd better take the first one we looked at today."

"I thought you weren't crazy about it."

"I'm not, but it appears I have unrealistic expectations. I wanted to find something this weekend, so I can get settled before I start teaching."

He pulled the car away from the curb. "Let's go get you that apartment, then."

Stephanie pulled out her phone. "I'm going to call to let them know I'll take it, and we're on our way to sign the papers."

"Good idea. Places get snapped up fast."

He merged into the left turn lane and waited for the arrow, listening to her end of the conversation.

"I guess we're not headed back there?"

"Nope. The person who looked at it, right after I did, leased it on the spot." She shoved her phone into her purse. "I'm sorry you

wasted another Sunday with me, looking for something that apparently doesn't exist."

"Nonsense," Dhruv said. "Your apartment is out there. You simply haven't found it yet."

"Maybe I need to look for something farther from the school where I'll be teaching. I'll just have a longer commute."

"Or maybe you'll find the perfect place in the next week or two."

"Aren't you sick of apartment hunting with me?"

"No. I like being with you. I don't care what we're doing. You didn't waste my time today."

"Thank you, Dhruv. I'd be at my wits' end without you."

"It's a sunny afternoon," he said. "They're predicting rain all next week. Why don't we pick up my dogs and take them and Biscuit out for a walk?"

"That's a great idea. I know she'd love the chance to stretch her legs. Are we going to take all four of your guys out?"

"I only have two now—a golden retriever and a dachshund. They're my dogs. I was fostering the other two. They've found

forever homes now."

"It's kind of you to do that."

"I love dogs." He parked at his apartment building. "Will Biscuit be okay with them?"

"She loves other dogs—as long as they're friendly."

"The golden is the most sweet-tempered dog I've ever had. The dachshund is bossy, but he'll be fine."

"Why didn't I meet them when I was there to play dominoes?"

"I took them upstairs, to my uncle's apartment. His kids—all six of them—love my dogs. His wife says she has her hands full and won't let them get a dog, so when one of the kids does something special, they're allowed to have my dogs for a sleepover."

Stephanie laughed. "Six kids? I don't blame her."

Dhruv led her to his apartment. A staccato series of barks started on the other side of the door when he inserted his key.

"That's Rocco—the dachshund." He pushed the door open and stepped inside. Rocco placed his front paws on Dhruv's pant leg while Sugar, the golden retriever, stood to one side, swishing her tail. "Sit. Stay," Dhruv commanded. The dogs obeyed. He stepped aside. "Would you like to come in?"

Stephanie and Biscuit entered Dhruv's apartment. She removed Biscuit's harness. "It's okay, girl. Would you like to make friends?"

Biscuit wagged her tail. She moved toward Sugar.

Sugar put her head down and her tail in the air. Biscuit extended her nose, and the two dogs politely sniffed each other.

Rocco trembled with excitement but didn't break his stay.

"Okay, Rocco. Break," Dhruv said.

The small dog inserted himself between Sugar and Biscuit and said his hello.

"I think they like each other," Dhruv cried.

"I agree."

"I'll get their leashes."

Stephanie slipped Biscuit's working harness on and they walked down the front steps to the sidewalk.

"Which way do you want to go?" Stephanie asked.

"Right," Dhruv replied. "I've got it all figured out."

"Really? Where're we going?"

"I thought we'd walk to your new school. You'll need to know how to find it."

"I'm not going to be living in this building, Dhruv. I probably won't find a place anywhere near here."

"You don't know that. There's still plenty of time." He put her hand on his elbow, and they started walking.

"Do you know where my school is?"

"Yep. Three of my uncle's kids go to it. I've been there numerous times for school concerts and sporting events." After half a block, he stopped and guided her to a large rectangular object. "This would be your closest landmark."

Stephanie reached out a hand and felt the sturdy metal box with the rounded top. "A mailbox?"

"Exactly."

"How do you know about landmarks?"

"Let's just say I've had experience with that."

He continued to lead her and Biscuit, pointing out a streetlight pole at an intersection and a fire hydrant along the way. "Here we are," he finally said. "The gate is locked because it's Sunday, but the main entrance is about fifty feet directly in front of us."

"That's an easy walk," Stephanie said. "I'd only have to cross one busy street. How long did that take us?"

"A little less than ten minutes."

"I wish something would open up in your building," she sighed wistfully. "It would be ideal for me."

"You never know what might happen."

She turned and reached for him.

He stepped awkwardly to her.

Stephanie put her arms around Dhruv.

He held her close.

"You're my rock, Dhruv," she whispered in his ear. "Thank you."

He drew back and hesitated, then leaned in and kissed her.

The slow, soft kiss increased in urgency. When they finally parted,

he cupped her face in his hands. "Don't give up. Something good is out there for you."

She nodded, brushing her cheek against his chest. Something—or someone—good was already there for her.

CHAPTER 60

"*N*ice to see you again, miss," the host said to Emily.

Connor turned to her. "Do you come to the Four Seasons often?"

Emily laughed. "Hardly. Garth and I were here earlier in the week. We met Gina for a drink."

"Right this way," the host said.

They followed him to their table.

A man stood as they approached. "You must be Emily," he said.

Emily extended her hand, and he shook it. "I've heard so much about you. It's nice to finally meet you. I can see why Connor was anxious to come back from Tokyo."

"Thank you," she said politely.

He continued to hold onto her hand. "I'm glad we have the chance to get to know each other."

Emily tugged gently on her hand, and he released it. Something about her husband's former boss rubbed her the wrong way.

They sat, and Garth slipped into place under the table.

"Do you always bring … your dog … with you?"

"Always," she replied curtly. She definitely didn't like this guy.

The waiter interrupted them to take their drink order. Connor and Gerald each ordered an expensive whiskey that the server described to them at some length. "For the lady? Might I interest you in one as well?"

"I'm fine with water," Emily said. "Whatever comes out of the tap. I won't be drinking."

"Very well," he said, removing the wine glass from in front of her.

"We're celebrating," Gerald said. "Won't you join us?"

"I'm happy with water."

"Of course," he said before snatching his handkerchief from the breast pocket of his suit coat and sneezing loudly. "I'm sorry," he sputtered. "I'm allergic to …" He sneezed again. "Dogs."

"Gosh, I'm so sorry about that," Emily said, trying to mean it.

"Let's order," Gerald said as the waiter placed their whiskeys in front of them.

The waiter listened attentively, asked a few questions, and departed.

"I'm always amazed that they remember orders without writing them down," Gerald said.

"There's a system to it," Connor said. "I've read about it. Waiters in all the high-end restaurants take great pride in never carrying an order pad."

Gerald raised his glass to Connor. "Here's to the person responsible for the most successful launch of a field office in the history of our company."

"Thank you," Connor said. They both sipped their whiskey.

"Congratulations, darling," Emily said. "I had no idea."

"Which brings me to why we're here tonight." Gerald placed his drink on the table. "The company wants to reinject itself into Europe. We got out of the region when the EU was in its infancy, but market studies now show that we can achieve record-breaking profit margins. Our analysts project our stock price will soar when we go back in."

"I've been reading about the success of US companies in the reinvigorated EU," Connor said. "Where do they plan to start?"

"France and Germany will be our initial targets, followed by Italy and Spain. An advance team has selected Paris as our European headquarters. They're close to signing a lease for office space."

"This is going to happen fast, isn't it?"

"All we need is someone to head up the newly established European division." He paused and took another sip of his whiskey. "That's why I'm here."

Emily stiffened.

"We'd like to offer you the position, Connor. The financial package is outstanding. The salary is double what you're making now, plus bonus and stock options. Not to mention you'd be living in the most beautiful city in the world." He turned to Emily. "Did I mention that the job comes with a company-provided apartment? We can make certain that it meets all of your accessibility requirements."

Emily could feel Connor tense in the chair next to her. He took another drink.

"Gosh ..." is all she could manage to say.

"I understand that you are a high-level programmer, Mrs. Harrington."

"It's Ms. Main. She didn't take my name." Connor upended his glass.

"Yes. Of course. I meant no offense." He signaled to the waiter to bring Connor another. "Our HR team would be happy to assist you in finding a new job—over there—if you'd like to continue working, although I'm sure you won't need to."

"I love my job," Emily said in measured tones. "I've worked very hard to return to it since ... since I lost my sight."

"We'll find something you like," Gerald said. He swung back to Connor. "This is a once-in-a-lifetime opportunity. What questions do you have?"

Connor accepted the second whiskey from the waiter and directed a series of questions to Gerald.

Emily slumped against the back of her chair. She knew the subject of living and working internationally would come up again, if she got back together with Connor. She just hadn't expected it to happen so soon.

She listened to her husband's discussion with Gerald. He was asking insightful questions; he was excited and engaged. And why shouldn't he be? He'd wanted this and worked hard for it his whole life. She couldn't resent Connor for that. He deserved this position. If she wanted their marriage to work, she had to make herself ready for this opportunity. Now.

Emily pushed back her chair and tugged on Garth's harness. "If you'll excuse me. I need to find the ladies' room."

Connor began to stand.

"No. Garth and I can find our way. You stay here and continue ..."

They had resumed their discussion before she'd left the table.

She entered the ladies' room and sank onto a stool in the anteroom. As the thick velvet upholstery cradled her, she inhaled a sweet, citrusy scent. There must be a candle burning nearby.

Garth sat at her feet.

She stroked his back. "What do you think, boy? Would you like to see Paris?" She was rubbing his ears when the phone rang in her purse, and the caller ID announced it was Mom.

Emily answered the call. She stood as she listened.

"I'm so sorry to hear this, Mom. I'm at dinner with Connor, but I'll pick up a few things at home and come right to the hospital."

She nodded as Martha continued to talk. "Traffic will be light by now. I'll be there in a couple of hours. Tell Zoe I'm on my way."

Emily's fingers flew across her screen as she ordered a rideshare. She grasped Garth's harness, and they made their way back to the table.

"I'm sorry," she said.

"What's wrong?" Connor asked.

"Irene's taken a turn for the worse. It's touch and go. She may not make it through the night."

"Oh, Em, I'm so sorry."

"I need to get to the hospital, Connor. Now."

He stood. "Of course." He turned to Gerald. "We'll have to continue this another time."

"No," Emily said. "I can go there on my own. I've already called

a car to pick me up." She faced Gerald. "It was nice to meet you. Connor is the right man for the job in Paris."

"Good luck to your friend," Gerald said.

"I'm going to come with you," Connor reiterated.

"No. I'm fine on my own. I can do this, Connor."

"At least let me see you to your car. I'll be back," he said to Gerald.

They rode the elevator to street level.

"Your car is pulling up now." He led her to the car and opened the door for her. "I should be driving you out there."

"You've had too much to drink to be driving tonight," Emily said. "Promise me you'll get a ride home."

"You're right. Don't worry."

"You should take the job, Connor. You've earned it."

"I'm intrigued—I have to admit it—but I'm not going to accept anything until we've had a chance to talk about it. I'm not going to make that mistake again." He leaned down and kissed her. "Call me when you get there, okay?"

"I will." She swung her feet into the car. "Congratulations. I'm proud of you," she said as Connor shut the door.

CHAPTER 61

*E*mily called Martha as soon as the car pulled up to the hospital entrance. "I'm downstairs."

"Good timing," Martha replied. "Zoe's here with me. They just made us leave Irene's room." She paused, and Emily knew she was choosing her words carefully because of Zoe. "They needed to go in to help Irene."

"Oh, God."

"We'll come right out to get you."

"I'll be in the lobby."

The rideshare driver had unloaded her backpack and the rolling suitcase that she'd hastily packed with a change of clothes and Garth's food. "I'll take these inside for you," he said. "Do you want me to wait with you?"

"Thank you, but I can manage." She reached out with her right arm.

He slipped the backpack onto her shoulder and placed the handle of her rolling suitcase within reach.

"Find the door," she commanded Garth, who took her

inside. She texted Connor that she had made it to the hospital. They were

approaching the reception desk when Martha called to her.

Emily turned toward the sound, and Zoe raced up to her,

throwing herself into Emily's arms. Emily held the little girl tightly as she began to sob.

"Gramma's dying." Zoe choked out the words.

Emily stroked her hair. "I'm so sorry, sweetheart."

Martha put her arms around both of their shoulders. "Zoe— can you take Emily to your grandmother's room? Do you remember how to get there?"

Zoe lifted her chin and nodded.

"I'm going to put Emily's suitcase and backpack in my car. You two go on ahead, and I'll be five minutes behind you."

"Thanks, Mom," Emily said.

"Check in at the nurse's station when you get there," Martha said. "They're expecting you."

Martha hurried through the front doors while Zoe and Emily made their way along the quiet corridors to a large set of double doors.

"Where are we?" Emily asked.

"The sign says Cardiac ICU," Zoe replied. She pushed a button on the wall, and the doors swung open slowly. "Gramma's room number is CI-207. It's on the other side of the hallway. The nurse's station is in the center. There's a big cart right outside her door."

"Take me there."

The ward was quiet, in the middle of the night, except for one room. Emily was aware that people were coming and going with speed and purpose. She assumed Irene's room was the center of all of the activity.

A woman coming out of Irene's room stopped abruptly and turned to Zoe and Emily. "Are you Emily?"

"I am."

"She's been waiting for you," the nurse said. "There's something she needs to say to you."

Emily's heart hammered in her chest. She'd spent the long car ride to the hospital praying that the crisis would pass—that Irene would survive.

"I'll take you in," the woman said.

Another nurse joined them. "I'll bring Zoe to our waiting room. You can sit with your grandmother's friend."

"She's not there," Emily said.

"Then I'll wait with Zoe," the nurse said, taking Zoe's hand.

Zoe pulled her hand back. "Can't I go with Emily?"

"I'm afraid that your grandmother is very ill," the nurse began.

Emily turned back, her mind racing. What would she have wanted if she'd been in Zoe's shoes? She placed her hand on Zoe's shoulder and felt the resolve in the little girl. "Your grandmother may die, Zoe. Do you want to be there when she does?"

"Will it be scary? Will she be in pain?"

Emily bit her lip. She'd never been with anyone at the moment
of their death.

"She won't be in any pain," the nurse answered. "Your grandmother is at peace with her death. She doesn't want to leave you," she added hastily, "but she's ready. I've seen a lot of people pass during my time as a nurse. It's not scary. I think it's nice when family members can see their loved ones go on."

"I want to be with Gramma," Zoe said. "Will you stay
with me, Emily?"

"Of course I will."

"Let's get the two of you to the bedside," the nurse said. She led them into the room. Irene's small form was dwarfed by the large hospital bed with tubes and wires running like leashes to monitors that flashed and beeped.

Zoe crowded in front of Emily as Garth positioned himself next to Zoe and sat.

"Emily's here," the nurse said. "Zoe and Emily are on your left side."

Irene's eyelids fluttered.

The nurse reached across the bed and placed Emily's hand over Irene's.

"I'm right here," Emily said. She felt a gentle pressure from Irene's hand.

The lines on the monitors remained steady.

Irene's lips began to move.

"She's trying to say something to you," the nurse said.

Emily cautiously lowered her face until her ear was over Irene's lips.

"Attorney has the papers. All set."

"Yes. I got a call from her office," Emily replied quietly.

"You'll take care of our Zoe? I ... can't."

"Yes. I love her with all my heart." Emily choked on the words. "I promise you; I'll do everything ..."

Irene pulled her hand away from Emily and waggled her fingers at Zoe.

Zoe bent her tear-stained face to her grandmother.

"Emily will take care of you now. You're a remarkable girl, and I'm proud of you." Irene placed a feathery kiss on the moist cheek. "I love you."

"Love ... you ... Gramma."

The heart rate monitor started a gradual decline. Zoe sank

back against Emily, who wrapped the trembling girl in her arms. They stood quietly at the bedside as the beeping subsided.

Irene took her final breath.

The nurse turned off the intrusive medical equipment. She consulted her watch and announced the time of death.

"You can stay here, with her, as long as you want," she said.

Zoe and Emily embraced each other and hung on tight.

"Would you go see if my mom—Martha—is in the waiting room?" she asked the nurse.

"I'm here," Martha said. "You didn't hear me come in." Her voice was thick with emotion.

Zoe pulled back and gazed at her grandmother. "She's not here, now." She spoke in a reverent whisper. "I saw her spirit leave her body. It looked like a puff of white smoke."

"I've heard a lot of people say that," the nurse said.

"I'm glad I was here." Zoe snuffled loudly. "I want to go home, now," she said, choking on the words.

Emily grasped Garth's harness with her left hand.

Zoe moved to Emily's right side and put her arm around Emily's waist. Emily took Martha's hand, and the three generations of women, now one family, left the hospital.

CHAPTER 62

$\mathcal{M}$y people were all profoundly sad. I'd been around Emily when she'd been serious—even short-tempered—but Zoe had always been a ball of energy. I hadn't expected this. I had my hands full.

We pulled into Martha's driveway and wearily climbed the steps to the front door. The barking that had started the minute the first car door had slammed shut increased in volume. I recognized that voice. My friend Sabrina was on the other side of the door.

We walked in, and Sabrina made a beeline for Zoe. She sniffed and licked the little girl's face.

"Why don't you go put your pajamas on?" Emily said. "I'll let Sabrina and Garth go outside; then I'll come in to say goodnight."

"What if I can't go to sleep?" Zoe asked in a small voice.

"Then I'll lie down with you until you do."

"Am I going to school tomorrow?"

"No," Emily said as she walked to the kitchen door. "I'm not going to work, either."

"I'll call the school," Martha said. "Let them know you won't be back until after … later."

Emily opened the door, and we dutifully went outside and did our business. Sabrina didn't try to chase me around the yard. She didn't want to play. I looked into her eyes as we stood, waiting to be let back in. She knew something was terribly wrong with our humans—and that we had a big part to play in bringing them comfort. We nodded to each other and waited.

Martha finally let us in.

Sabrina headed straight for Zoe's bedroom. The little girl was balled up under the covers, crying into her pillow. Sabrina forced her way into Zoe's arms and sprawled against her chest.

Emily lay across the foot of the bed, her legs dangling off the side. I sat next to her. She rested a hand on top of my head, patting me intermittently.

Zoe's breathing progressed from jerky sobs to deep, steady breaths. Emily continued to lay at her feet, long after Zoe had gone to sleep. I could tell from the way she was breathing that

Emily was thinking.

She finally pushed herself slowly into a sitting position. We crept out of Zoe's room. She pulled the door halfway shut behind her.

We went down the hallway to the kitchen.

Martha sat at the table, pouring through papers spread out in front of her.

"Mom?" Emily's voice was soft.

"Is she finally asleep?"

"Yes. She quieted down a while ago—maybe twenty minutes

—I stayed with her just to make sure. I've left her door open, so I can hear if she wakes up or calls for me."

Martha smiled. "You're going to be a great mother to that little girl, Em."

"I've had the perfect role model." Emily pulled out a chair and sat with Martha. "What're you doing?"

"Irene and I talked about her funeral a couple of weeks ago. I know what she wants. She also prepaid for her burial expenses. I'm going through all of that paperwork." She sank against the back of her chair. "I couldn't get to sleep, so I thought I'd do something productive. This is going to be a hectic time for you, Em. I thought I'd take care of all of this if you don't mind."

"I hadn't considered those arrangements," Emily said. "I'd be grateful if you did. I've been thinking about Zoe."

"You've taken on a lot," Martha said. "At a time when you're still adjusting to being blind. I'm sorry all of this is hitting you at once, but I'm proud of you, too. I know you can handle anything that comes your way. And I'm here to help."

"You always are, Mom. I'm so grateful." She placed her elbows on the table and put her head in her hands. "Everything's such a jumble. I was just getting used to my apartment, but it's too small for Zoe and me. There's always Irene's house —Irene told me she had left it to Zoe in trust—but I'm familiar with *your* house. Could we stay here—with you—until the end of the school year?"

"You're more than welcome—both of you—but wouldn't that make an awfully long commute to work for you?"

"I know," Emily agreed. "I could do it for a while, but I'd want us to move back into the city. It's probably best for Zoe to wait until after the end of the school year."

"I don't think she's happy at her school. She doesn't have

any friends there, and there are no kids on this block. She might be excited to move."

"You think?"

"I do. It's something to consider."

"I'll talk to her about it," Emily said. "After the funeral."

"What about Connor? I know that you've been seeing each other to find out if you can make a go of your marriage."

Emily's head sunk closer to the table. "I don't know. He was upset with me when I agreed to be Zoe's guardian. We had a big fight. He was mad that I hadn't talked to him before agreeing to it." She clawed a hand through her tangled hair. "He was right to be mad. We pushed the issue aside because Irene hadn't died —and we didn't think she would."

"And now she has," Martha said.

"The thing is, Mom, it wouldn't have mattered if Connor didn't want me to be her guardian. I would have said yes, even if he didn't agree. Zoe is more important to me than he is."

Martha sat in silence, taking this in.

"That's hugely telling, isn't it? Shouldn't I be more concerned about what he wants?"

"How will you know what he wants without asking him?"

"I don't have to ask him. I already know. He may deny it, but his dream life involves living and working—in Paris."

"I haven't heard this before."

"We were at dinner with his old boss when you called. They're

offering Connor the chance to lead a new European division, with headquarters in Paris and a swanky, company-owned apartment.

The financial package is incredible, and they'll help me find a new

job over there."

"Wow. That does sound like a dream come true."

"It is for him. I listened to him discuss the opportunity with Gerald. Every fiber of his being was alive with excitement. At one time in my life, I would have been right there with him." She blew out a long breath. "But not anymore. I want to stay here, in my current job, and continue to learn braille and hone my skills. That's even before we consider Zoe's needs. I don't want Paris, Mom."

"Did Connor accept the job?"

"No. He told Gerald he'd have to think about it and talk to me. I left in the middle of dinner. Connor walked me to the car, and I told him that he should take it."

"What did he say?"

"That we'd need to talk."

"So, talk to him, Em. Listen to what he says. Don't make up his mind for him. Maybe he'll understand and be happy to stay here."

"He might be willing to do that, but it wouldn't be right for him. I know what I need to do."

"Don't decide tonight," Martha said. "You can't be thinking clearly. Get a good night's sleep—a couple of good nights' sleep —and then talk to him."

Emily stood. "That's good advice. I'm completely out of gas. Come on, Garth. Let's go to bed."

CHAPTER 63

*E*mily came out of her bedroom, rubbing her hair vigorously with a towel. She'd only slept a few hours but had given up trying to fall back to sleep when she'd awakened at her usual time. Her mind was racing with all of the decisions she had to make.

The sofa creaked as someone lifted themselves out of it.

"Mom?"

"No. It's me, Em."

"Connor? What are you doing here?"

"I called the house first thing. Martha told me that Irene died." He crossed to her and took her in his arms. "I'm so sorry."

"I didn't want to wake you in the middle of the night. I got a few hours of sleep and was just about to call you."

"It's okay. I'm here now. That's all that matters."

Emily stepped out of his embrace. "You took off work. I wasn't expecting that."

"I thought you'd need me."

"That was nice. How long have you been here?"

"Not long. Fifteen minutes."

"Where's Mom?"

"She went to lay down right after I got here."

"Zoe?"

"Martha checked on her. She's still asleep."

"Let's go out back," Emily said, "where we can talk without disturbing them."

She made her way to an upholstered chair on the patio.

"You don't have your cane," Connor remarked. "But you didn't need it. I'd never have guessed that you can't see where you were going."

"Blind people become very acclimated to their environ-ments," Emily said. "Muscle memory, and all that."

He lowered himself into the chair next to her. A car crept down the street, and they heard the thump of the morning newspaper hitting a driveway.

"How did the rest of the meeting go?"

"You mean last night? With Gerald?"

"Yes. It's hard to think that it was less than twenty-four hours ago." She tucked her feet up under herself. "He's made you a wonderful offer, Connor."

"Yes." He inhaled deeply and continued slowly. "I'm glad that you feel that way."

"It's perfect for you, Connor."

"It's perfect for both of us. Paris is almost too good to be true. Now that you've become so accomplished in your adapta-tion to blindness, you'll be fine. You can continue working from there. If you need to find a new job, our HR department will help you. Gerald and I talked a lot more about that. Wait until I tell you …"

"Stop." Emily held up her hand to emphasize her point. "Paris is perfect for you, but not for me."

Connor blew out a breath. "Because you now have to take care of Zoe?"

Emily winced as he said it.

"I've been thinking about that," he continued. "We could take her with us. Think about what a wonderful opportunity that would be for her. And with my salary, we could send her to the most exclusive English-speaking school in the city. I was doing some research on my phone while I was waiting for you to get out of the shower."

"All of that may be true, Connor, but I don't want to disrupt my life right now."

"You agreed to disrupt your life by becoming her guardian," he retorted.

Emily turned away from him.

"Then we won't go to Paris. I'll turn the job down."

"No, Connor. *No.* I don't want you to do that. It's not fair to you. I saw how you came alive last night, making plans for a new European division. If you turn it down, you'll always resent me—and Zoe."

"Maybe in a year or two, you'll be ready to go with me." He scooted his chair toward hers and leaned his elbows on his knees. "I could go over on my own and see you when I'm back here. I'll have meetings at the home office. The two of you could come for an extended vacation this summer. We could see what Zoe thinks of the idea of moving to Paris."

"I don't think a long-distance relationship is what we need…"

"No. Hear me out." He was talking fast, gesturing with his hands. "It could work—you know it could. We can Skype and Zoom—all of that. Military families do it all the time."

"It's more than that. We want different things now. My relationship with Zoe has shown me that I want more children."

The chair creaked as he rose and began to pace. "So now you want a baby? We always said that we didn't want kids. I feel like this sudden interest in motherhood is coming out of left field." His voice took on a harsh tone. "How on earth—*now*—do you expect to cope with an infant?"

She recoiled at his words. "You mean because I'm blind?"

He raised his palms and shrugged. "I guess we could hire a live-in nanny."

"Damn it, Connor! I don't want and won't need a nanny. Lots of blind people—*blind couples*—have children and do just fine." A leaf blower started up in the yard behind them. She raised her voice to be heard over the din. "I need you to believe in me. If you can't see me as capable, how am I ever going to see myself that way?"

"Looks like I'm back to saying all the wrong things, again."

"That's not it. We simply don't work anymore. I agreed to become Zoe's guardian without consulting you because I would have said *yes* no matter what you thought." She pressed her palms against her thighs and forced herself to continue. "That's not fair to you. I understand you might feel blindsided by my interest in starting a family, but I can assure you—it's real."

He knelt next to her chair.

"You're a wonderful man, Connor. I love you for coming back—for the sacrifice you made—to see if our marriage could work.

You deserve someone who'll support *your* hopes and dreams. I'm

so sorry, but that's not me. Not anymore. If I let you turn down this big opportunity, you'll regret it." She reached out and touched his face. A tear found her fingers. "I love you, Connor, but this is best for both of us."

He nodded his head slowly. "I wanted us to work, Em. I wanted the old *us*. I guess that doesn't exist anymore."

She was crying softly. "I don't think it does." She pressed her forehead against his, their breath hot on each other's cheeks.

"If you're certain. I don't want to desert you when you need me—again."

"I'm positive. Go home. Now. Before Zoe wakes up. She doesn't need to think about any of this."

He nodded and got to his feet, pulling her up with him.

"I'll always love you, Em. I hope you get what you want out of life. You deserve it. I still feel responsible for that damned accident."

"That was not your fault. Stop feeling guilty about it. As time goes by, I'm realizing more and more that things have been added to my life because I lost my sight."

"You remain the bravest person I know."

She stood on her tiptoes and kissed him gently. "Go set Europe on fire, Connor."

He nodded and trudged around the house to his car.

Emily stood in the backyard, arms around herself, until long after the sound of his car had faded. She decided to follow her heart. It was time to plan a future for Zoe, Sabrina, Garth, and herself.

CHAPTER 64

*E*mily stood, one arm around Zoe's shoulders, as people filed past them, shaking hands and murmuring in comforting tones. I sat next to them, chin up and alert. We were in a sunny room with a high ceiling. A long table in the center held trays of food. After people spoke to us, they put food on plates and sat together at round tables dotted around the room. The conversation was light and cheerful, punctuated with laughter—a sharp contrast to the somber voices and soft crying of these same humans not more than half an hour ago in a room with rows of benches, a loud organ, and colored windows.

I was sad that we'd had to leave Sabrina at home. I would have loved her take on this thing called a funeral.

I lifted my nose in the air and sniffed. Chanel No. 5. Gina was here somewhere. I looked for her but couldn't see her through the people in front of us. I didn't have long to wait.

"Hey, Zoe," Gina said, leaning over and sweeping the girl into her arms. "I'm so sorry."

"Gina. You came," Emily said.

"Of course I did."

"That was nice of you."

"I had to be here … for my girls." She touched Zoe's shoulder. "You've been very brave. Your grandmother and your parents would be so proud of you."

"Thanks," Zoe said.

"She's been mature beyond her years," Emily agreed.

"I've taken the afternoon off. I told Martha I'd stay to help her put the food away and clean up."

"I appreciate that," Emily said. "The food smells good. Get some for yourself."

"I'm going to do that right now. I'll fix both of you plates and set them aside. Are you hungry, Zoe?"

Zoe nodded.

"I'm on it," Gina said. "And if there's anything else I can do for you—anything at all—you just let me know."

"Will do," Emily said as Gina stepped away.

I turned my attention back to the line. People just kept on coming. I stretched my back, then resumed my alert posture. If Emily and Zoe could stand here, I could sit.

The line began to thin out, and my heart leaped at the sight at the end of the receiving line. I blinked. My eyes weren't deceiving me. The last two people waiting to pay their respects were Dhruv and Stephanie. And there was my friend Biscuit.

"Dhruv," Zoe cried, throwing her arms out to him.

He leaned down and hugged her.

"I didn't expect to see you, Dhruv."

"I wanted to be here," he replied. "I've brought Stephanie, too."

"I'm glad you both came," Emily said.

"It was a beautiful service," Stephanie said. "I know people always say that, but it really was."

"A lot of people loved your grandmother," Dhruv said to Zoe.

"Irene was very special," Emily agreed. "How are things going for you, Stephanie? When do you start your new job?"

"I report on Monday to begin shadowing the teacher I'm going to take over for. She'll be on maternity leave in three weeks unless the baby comes early. Dhruv and I are going to the classroom tomorrow afternoon so I can get acclimated to it and to make things accessible."

"How exciting. Have you found a place to live yet?"

"No—and I've been looking like crazy. Dhruv's been helping me. There's nothing out there." She sighed heavily. "I'm going to commute from my mom's until I can find something."

"You'll get a place," Dhruv stated matter-of-factly. "It just hasn't happened yet."

"Ahhh ... he's the eternal optimist, isn't he?" Stephanie said playfully.

"I've got my fingers crossed," Emily said. Zoe sagged against her side. "Have something to eat. Mom's got enough food to feed an army."

Biscuit turned her head to me as they walked by and winked. I nodded in return. She must have understood how hard I had been working lately, pouring comforting dog pheromones on my people.

"Are you hanging in there, sweetie?" Emily asked Zoe. "It's been an emotional morning. I'm so proud of you."

"I cried during the funeral," Zoe said. "I cried a lot."

"Me, too. And that's okay. It's normal."

"Will all the heavy sadness go away?" Zoe transferred a wadded-up tissue from hand to hand.

"It will—it takes time." Emily extended her palm for the soggy tissue. Zoe gave it to her, and Emily placed it in her pocket. "Crying makes me exhausted. Are you tired?"

Zoe nodded, brushing her cheek against Emily's side.

"Do you want to go home?"

Zoe nodded again.

"Can you find Gina? Let's ask her to give us a ride. We can take our lunch with us."

"She's talking to your mom. Follow me."

I got to my feet and followed Zoe before Emily even gave the command.

We were home, and they were nestled on the couch in no time. Styrofoam boxes containing cold cuts, pasta salad, and fruit lay open on the coffee table in front of us.

Sabrina sprawled on the sofa, her head in Zoe's lap. I was content to lie at Emily's feet.

"Would you like to watch a movie?" Emily asked.

Zoe got up and riffled through the black plastic boxes that lived in a basket next to the television. We'd been watching a lot of TV since we'd come home from the hospital. Zoe's favorite was *Beauty and the Beast*. I bet we'd seen it half a dozen times. It wasn't a bad movie, of course, but the scenes in the woods— with the wolves—were a bit dark and scary for my taste. Despite the wildebeests and hyenas, I preferred *The Lion King*— especially that Timon character. He was my favorite.

"How about this one? *101 Dalmatians*," Zoe said.

My ears perked up. There was *another* movie about dogs? I loved *Lady and the Tramp*.

"I haven't seen that one in years. Good choice."

Zoe started the movie, and I scooted over, so I had an unobstructed view of the screen.

Later that night, as Emily and I were tucking Zoe and

Sabrina into bed, Emily smoothed Zoe's silky hair off her face. "Tomorrow is Saturday, and it's been a hard week," she said. "I need to study my braille, and I know you have schoolwork to make up, but we can do that on Sunday. Let's have some fun. What would you like to do?"

"Can we go to your apartment?"

"Of course we can, but what's fun for you to do there?"

"I think I want to be someplace different," Zoe said. "I feel Gramma all the time, here."

"I understand that. We'll leave in the morning."

"Can I go with Stephanie and Dhruv to her classroom? I helped you set up your apartment. I know what to do."

"You'd be great at it," Emily said. "That's so thoughtful of you."

"It'll be fun. I like them."

"They like you." She leaned over and kissed Zoe on the forehead. "I'll call them now. Sweet dreams, sweet girl. We've got a big day tomorrow."

CHAPTER 65

"They're here," Martha called over her shoulder as she opened the door.

Emily, Garth, and Zoe stepped onto the porch.

"You girls have fun," Martha said. "Let me know if you change your minds and want me to come get you."

"We'll be fine," Emily said. "You're going to have all of us under foot for quite a while, so enjoy some peace."

"I love having you here."

"What do you plan to do today?" Emily asked as her mother leaned in and kissed her on the cheek.

"I'm going to weed my garden this morning—it's a complete mess. I may take a nap after lunch."

"I approve." Emily chuckled. "Especially the part about that nap. You need it."

"You'd better get going."

"See you Sunday afternoon," Emily said as she and Garth

followed Zoe to their rideshare. The three of them piled into the backseat.

"Did Stephanie really say she wanted me to help?" Zoe asked.

"Absolutely! She's stayed at my place, remember? She knows how well it's set up—thanks to you. She jumped at the chance when I talked to her last night."

"Cool," Zoe said.

"You've got to do what she says," Emily continued. "This is her classroom. You're there to do what she wants."

"I know," Zoe said. "Is this the elementary school closest to your apartment?"

"It is. Stephanie went there as a child." Emily settled into her seat. "We'll be there in no time," she said. "Traffic is light. Are you sure you don't want me to come with you?"

"Nope," Zoe said, shaking her head vigorously. "I'm fine with Dhruv and Stephanie. And Biscuit."

"I'll pack up the things I'm going to need, now that I'll be living at Mom's again."

"Are we going to live with your mom forever?"

"No. Maybe until the end of the school year? Would you rather stay in your grandmother's house? You'll own it when you're older."

"No! I don't want that house." Zoe's voice cracked. "It makes me sad to see it every day."

"You may change your mind about that when you're older. We won't live there now."

"I like your apartment," Zoe said.

"I do too, but a studio is too small for both of us and two dogs. There's not even enough room for your bed."

"I like sleeping on the sofa."

Emily leaned across the seat and rubbed Zoe's back. "Don't worry about all of this. We've got plenty of time to make decisions. Right now, we both need to concentrate on getting caught up on our schoolwork. I'm going to see your grandmother's attorney on Tuesday. We'll get back into a routine, and that'll make us both feel better."

Zoe turned to the window and watched as they crossed the bridge and into the city.

They had just entered the lobby of Emily's building when Dhruv, Stephanie, and Biscuit stepped out of his apartment.

"We saw you get out of the car," Dhruv said. "When you're ready, we thought we'd walk to the school. Stephanie and Biscuit will lead the way."

"Neat!" Zoe said.

"I'm going to stay here," Emily said. "Is that all right?"

"Absolutely," Stephanie said. "We'll be back by dinnertime."

"Why don't I take us all to the Thai place for dinner?" Dhruv suggested.

"I'd love that. Thank you, Dhruv. Do you like Thai food, Zoe?"

"I've never had it."

"You can try it," Dhruv said. "If you don't like it, I have hot dogs at my house."

"Have fun, guys," Emily said. "I'll be here. Call me if you need me, Zoe."

"I'll be fine," Zoe said, and Emily swore she could hear the little girl roll her eyes.

**

Later that night, after Zoe had discovered that she loved

Thai food *and* that she could beat the adults at dominoes, she and Emily pulled on their pajamas.

Zoe curled up on the sofa, and Emily tucked the thick duvet that usually lived on Emily's bed around Zoe. "Stephanie was very grateful for your help," she said. "She couldn't stop talking about you. Did you have fun?"

"So much fun! We walked all around the school when we were done in her room. The art room is way bigger than the one at my school. They have band, too. We don't have that at my school. Not until seventh grade."

"I'm so excited for Stephanie."

"She's nervous, I can tell."

"That's the way it is with new jobs. Once you get started, your nerves go away."

"Like if I changed schools? I'd be scared at first, but it'd go away?"

"Exactly." Emily leaned down and kissed her forehead.

"Emily?"

"What, honey?"

"I miss Sabrina."

"Would you like to put Garth's bed next to the sofa?"

"Will he mind?"

Emily chuckled. "No. Garth can sleep anywhere."

Zoe jumped up and repositioned Garth's bed. She slipped back under the duvet.

Emily got into bed and nestled against her pillow.

"Emily?"

Emily propped herself on her elbow.

"Yes?"

"Could I switch schools? To Stephanie's school. We could live here?"

"Oh, honey ... I don't know."

"You'd be close to work. I could walk to school. You wouldn't have to take me."

"This apartment is too small for us," Emily reminded her. "We'd need to find somewhere new to live. I'd have to see if you could enroll in the school. Maybe this fall. There's been enough change for you lately. Finish out the school year where you are." She laid back down.

"Emily?"

Emily remained silent.

"I'd be scared to change, but it'd go away. You just said so."

Emily put her hand on her forehead. She was beginning to see why people said parenting could be so hard.

"I want to change now. This year. We can stay here until you find us a bigger place. It's better for your job."

A smile crept across Emily's face. Between Dhruv and Zoe, she had two of the most persistent people on the planet in her life.

"Let me think about it," Emily said. "We'll talk more about it

in the morning."

"Emily," Zoe called one last time. "I love you."

***

Emily lay awake until she heard Zoe's rhythmic breathing from the sofa. She turned her covers back and took her phone into the bathroom, carefully shutting the door behind her.

She dictated a text to Stephanie: "Zoe would like to transfer schools. Do you know if I can enroll her?"

Emily poured herself a glass of water, and the response came before she could finish drinking it.

"I'm sure she could. I'll talk to the woman I'm taking over

267

for tomorrow morning and ask her how to do it. I'll call you as soon as I know."

"You're the best," Emily replied.

She brought her phone to her mouth. She had one more text to send. With any luck, she'd be able to wake up Zoe with the news that she could grant her wish.

CHAPTER 66

*D*hruv was waiting for Emily and Garth when they got off the elevator the next morning.

"Where's Zoe?"

"She's eating her breakfast and watching cartoons. I don't want to get her hopes up unless I know I can make this work."

"Did you hear from Stephanie?"

"Yes. I can enroll Zoe whenever. They have room in two of their fourth-grade classes. That just leaves finding us a bigger place to live. You mentioned that your uncle had a two-bedroom in this building. Is it still available?"

"No."

"Shoot. Now I'll have to start looking for an apartment. With everything going on in my life right now, I don't know how I'm going to do it."

"You won't have to."

"What do you mean?"

"There's a three-bedroom, two-bath unit on the first floor.

My uncle is having it painted now. It's the second biggest one in the building."

"Really?"

"I can get the key from him and let you see it this afternoon."

"Tell me about it."

"The kitchen has all the same appliances that you have. It's bigger, with more cabinets and counter space. The master bedroom has an attached bathroom, and there's a Jack and Jill bath between the other bedrooms."

"That sounds ideal for us."

"One of the bedrooms has built-in, floor-to-ceiling shelves."

"Zoe could put her books and stuffed animals there. And my mom could have her own bedroom. I think she'd like to come into the city and stay with us from time to time. She could attend lectures at the art museum and take classes at some of the galleries. She's always wanted to do that. How much is it?"

"A thousand a month more than what you're paying for your studio."

"I can afford that." She inhaled sharply. "What about Stephanie? She needs a place."

"It's too big, and she can't afford it on a teacher's salary."

Emily's head jerked up. "That's it! The perfect solution you're always talking about."

"I was wondering," Dhruv said, and she could hear the smile in his voice.

"Call your uncle and tell him to put my name on that lease.

And tell Stephanie that a studio in this building is coming available." She and Garth turned back to the elevator. "Let her know she can stay there until the current resident moves downstairs," she called over her shoulder.

∗∗∗

Emily burst into her apartment. "Zoe. Turn off the TV—we need to talk."

Zoe did as she was told. "What's up? Am I in trouble?"

"Nothing of the kind. I was talking to Dhruv and Stephanie while you were asleep. I need you to listen to me very carefully and think about your answers. Once we make this decision, we have to stick with it."

Zoe sat and curled her legs beneath her. "Okay."

Emily took a deep breath before she began. "I can enroll you in the school near here right away. We can move to a big, three-bedroom apartment on the first floor of this building. There'll be plenty of room for Garth and Sabrina. And there's a room for Mom when she wants to visit."

"Like we have bedrooms at her house?" Zoe was bouncing with excitement.

"Exactly. And Stephanie can move in here, so you could walk to school with her."

Zoe clapped her hands.

"You need to be certain. Is this what you want to do? I'll have to sign a lease for the apartment. Once I do, there's no going back."

"I'm sure. Pinky swear," she said, hooking Emily's pinky finger with her own.

Emily laughed. "Let's do this thing. We'll need to go back to Mom's for a few weeks until I get all the paperwork done and the apartment downstairs is ready. I'm going to let Stephanie stay here until we move out and she moves in."

"I'm so excited," Zoe said. "I think we should clean this place up—for Stephanie."

"Good idea," Emily said. "I'll strip my bed and start my sheets in the washer." She tapped her phone, which told her it was nine ten.

"Let's start in on our homework and work like mad until lunchtime. After we eat, we'll get this place ready for Stephanie. I'll tell her she can pick up the key from Dhruv. Let's plan to be done and headed for home by three. How does that sound?"

"We can do it," Zoe said, leaping off the sofa and dragging her backpack onto the coffee table. "I have two math worksheets and three chapters in the book we're reading for English."

Emily sat down at the kitchen table with her laptop and her brailler and began working. By the time they broke for lunch, they each reported that they were caught up on their studies.

They walked to a sandwich shop on the corner for a quick bite to eat. By the time they returned to the apartment, it was almost one thirty.

"We'd better get cracking," Emily said. "I'll make my bed and clean the bathroom. Can you dust and vacuum?"

"I used to do that for Gramma. I know how."

They set themselves to their tasks, and Emily almost didn't hear her phone ringing over the din of the vacuum cleaner. The caller ID announced it was Gina.

"Hey!" Emily said, tapping the screen.

"You sound out of breath. Did I catch you at a bad time?"

"Not at all. Zoe and I are cleaning my apartment."

"Are you in town?" Gina chuckled. "I guess that's a silly question. How else could you be cleaning your apartment? Why are you here? I thought you were going to stay with Martha for the time being."

"Change of plans," Emily said. "We're moving back to the city—into a three-bedroom in my building. It won't be for a couple of weeks. We're cleaning my place because Stephanie is moving in later today."

"Whoa—slow down. I'll need to hear all the details. Can I come over?"

"There's not much more to tell."

"I've got something important to show you!"

"You got your ring?"

"We picked it up yesterday. I was calling to check on you—and to tell you about it."

"Get over here! I can't wait to see it. Do you remember where I live?"

"Of course I do. See you in fifteen." Gina hung up the phone, and Emily resumed scrubbing the tile in her shower. The bathroom smelled of Lysol. Stephanie would know they'd made an effort.

She was bagging up the trash, and Zoe was storing the vacuum in the closet when they heard the knock on the door.

"Gina?" Emily called.

"The one and only!"

Emily opened the door.

"Hey, guys," Gina said. "This place looks fabulous. Good job."

"Thank you. We worked so hard." Zoe twisted her body from side to side. "Emily says you're engaged, and she bets you've got 'quite a rock.'"

Gina laughed. "Once again, Emily is right. Or at least, I think she is." She held out her left hand to Zoe. "What do you think?"

"Wow! It's so big and sparkly. And blue."

"You got a sapphire? You always said that's what you wanted."

"Surrounded by diamonds. I picked out a much smaller stone than this. Craig insisted on seeing larger ones." She put her hand in Emily's. Emily led her to the kitchen and put her hand under the bright light above the kitchen sink. She positioned her left eye over her friend's ring finger, her cheek almost touching Gina's hand.

Gina held her breath and waited.

"There! I can see it." She moved her eye in a circle. "That's spectacular. The stone is such a deep blue. Is the setting like the one you cut out of that magazine when you were in high school and pinned to your bulletin board?"

"You remember all my guilty secrets, don't you? As a matter of fact, it is."

Emily stood. "Nothing wrong with that. If you still like it, all these years later, I don't think you'll ever get tired of it."

"I'd better not." She leaned against the counter. "So, fill me in."

"I wish I could, but we need to head back to Mom's. Can I call you this week?"

"How're you getting there?"

"We'll call a rideshare."

"No, you won't—I'm driving you."

"I don't want to put you out—that's a two-hour round trip."

"That's an hour to spend with my favorite gals," she said. "I have the time. You can tell me everything." She turned to Zoe. "What do you say, kiddo?"

"I think it's a great idea."

"Is this your stuff—by the door?"

"Yep. We're all ready to go. I just need to take Garth out back."

"We'll load the car while you and Garth do that." Gina picked up an armload of Emily's clothes, still on hangers. "Oh," she said. "I almost forgot. I also called to invite you to an engagement party that Craig's aunt is throwing for us at her home a week from Saturday. Cocktails at six, dinner at seven.

She lives in a very swanky neighborhood. Craig says the house is spectacular."

"I don't know …" Emily began.

"You should go!" Zoe said. "Will it be fancy?" she asked Gina. "Very."

"You can wear that dress you bought when we went shopping."

"Good point," Gina high-fived Zoe. "The one that she insisted she didn't need—that she'll now be wearing for the second time."

Emily held up both hands, laughing. "I give in. I'll go."

"Terrific. I can't wait for you to meet Craig, and he's dying to meet you. I talk about you all the time."

Emily picked up Garth's harness and placed it over his

head. "We'll meet you two in front. I'll give the key to Dhruv on my way out."

"Let's roll, ladies!" Gina cried.

CHAPTER 67

$\mathcal{I}$'d had a bath and a brush and knew I was looking my best. Emily had done the same, but she now sat motionless at the foot of her bed, the slinky green dress we'd bought spread out behind her. For some reason, she'd stalled.

"Come in," she said in response to the knock on her door.

Mom and Zoe hovered in the doorway.

"Your car's here," Zoe said.

"Do you need help with your dress?" Martha moved to the bed and removed the garment from its hanger.

"I don't know if I have the energy to go," Emily's shoulders slumped. "It's been such a busy couple of weeks."

What was she talking about? We'd spent most of our time sitting in one boring lawyer's office or another. First, we'd taken care of all of the guardianship paperwork for Zoe, and then we'd joined Connor for a session at the divorce lawyer.

They were having an amicable divorce. Connor had decided to sell the condo and move to Paris. He'd told Emily she could have everything in the condo if she wanted it. It turns out we did. We were moving into our big new apartment next weekend and would need all of that stuff.

I know I hadn't taken to Connor when I first met him, but he'd turned out to be a decent guy. They both seemed a little bit sad when they'd said goodbye outside of the lawyer's office. But the tilt in Emily's shoulders and the spring in her step as we walked away told me she was doing the right thing.

"Come on," Mom said. "Put your hands above your head."

"With the move to the new apartment next weekend, I think I need to stay home and rest," Emily said, her voice muffled by the dress as Martha pulled it over her head.

"Nonsense," Mom replied. "What you need is to get out and enjoy yourself."

Once more, I agreed wholeheartedly with Mom. It was time for us to move. I hadn't been on an adventure in longer than

I could remember.

"Stand up, and I'll zip you."

Emily complied.

"Wow," Zoe said.

"You look fabulous," Mom agreed. "Now—go have fun. And don't you dare come home before midnight."

"Yeah. You're not Cinderella," Zoe chimed in. "Nothing bad's going to happen to you."

Martha handed Emily a small, beaded purse.

Emily took my harness, and we set out. She sat in the back of the car with me, opening and closing the metal clasp on her purse with an annoying click. She was nervous. I rested my muzzle on her lap.

She patted the top of my head and moved it aside. "I don't want slobber on my dress, Garth."

I pulled my head back. Me—slobber? First I was hearing of

this. I moved to the other side of the backseat and stayed there for the rest of our journey.

We pulled up to a large home set back from the street by a wide strip of lush grass. I hoped I'd have the opportunity to roll in it before we left.

A cluster of uniformed people were parking cars. One of them opened our door and helped Emily out. I trailed behind as he escorted her to the door.

An attendant in a black dress and white apron handed Emily a glass of champagne. I smelled Chanel No. 5. Before I could make a move, Gina was upon us.

"Em!" Gina gushed. "You're here. I was worried you wouldn't show."

"Of course I'm here," Emily said. "I wouldn't dream of missing this." I cut my eyes to Emily. Now she was telling little white lies. She must be more nervous than I thought.

"You look absolutely stunning," Gina said. "If you weren't my best friend, I'd be jealous. Come on." She took Emily's elbow. "I can't wait for you to meet Craig."

Gina led us to a tall, tanned blond man wearing a tailored black suit, white shirt, and silver tie that almost matched the sparkly fabric of Gina's dress. They looked very handsome together—nearly as good as Emily and me.

"So, this is the person that Gina loves most in the world," he said, leaning over and taking Emily's hand in both of his.

"I think that honor falls to you," Emily replied.

"I'm afraid not," Craig said, "but I'm okay with that, as long as we can be friends, too."

Emily laughed. "I'm sure we will be."

I sat while they continued their banter. My eyelids were starting to grow heavy when a woman about Mom's age, wearing an elaborately jeweled dress and too much makeup, grabbed Craig's elbow.

"I'm sorry to interrupt," a woman who turned out to be Craig's aunt said in a way that showed she wasn't sorry. "I need to steal you two away. The buffet is ready, and I want you and Gina to be the first ones through it."

"Come with us," Craig said to Emily.

"No." Emily took a step back. "I need to find the powder room. I'll catch up with you later."

"It's on the left, at the end of the hall," the aunt said. She hadn't even noticed me.

"I'll come with you," Gina said.

"No way. Garth and I've got this."

Craig and Gina allowed themselves to be pulled toward an open set of French doors. The crowd of people around us followed them.

"Find me a chair," Emily said.

I looked around. There were lots of chairs to choose from. An arched doorway at the other end of the room revealed a hearth with a welcoming fire. A tall, leather wing-backed chair stood to one side of it. That looked like a comfortable place for us to rest.

I took us to the chair. Not until we'd entered the room did I see the matching chair on the other side of the fire—and the lanky, tanned blond man sitting in it. He was almost an identical copy of Craig.

Emily sat and extended her legs in front of her. She slipped her feet out of her shoes.

I sat next to her and eyed the man.

"It's hard to be on your feet at these things, isn't it?"

Emily startled. "Oh … I didn't realize …"

"I'm sorry," he said. "I should have spoken sooner. I'm Grant Johnson—Craig's twin brother."

Emily extended her hand to him, and he leaned over and took it in his own.

"Emily Main," she said.

"I thought you must be. I've heard so much about you from Gina."

"I hope that's a good thing."

"Believe me. It's all good."

"Shouldn't you join the others—for dinner?"

"To tell you the truth, I've had a tough week. I just don't have the energy. I was enjoying sitting here, by the fire."

Emily turned her palm toward the warmth of the flames. "It is nice, isn't it? I'll bet this is a beautiful house."

"It certainly is. Would you like me to describe it for you?"

"I'd love that."

"It's a big house—it'll take some time. I have to warn you—I'm an architect. Once I get started, you may not be able to shut me up."

Emily laughed. "Sounds perfect to me."

"Why don't I get us both something to eat? I'll be right back, and I can tell you all you want to know."

Grant returned, juggling four plates. He set them on a low, round table, which he pulled up to Emily. He took napkins wrapped around silverware from the breast pocket of his jacket and placed a set up in Emily's hand. "I see you have a glass of champagne. I snagged water bottles from the kitchen. My aunt would kill me if she saw us with plastic bottles, but I won't tell if you don't." He unscrewed the bottle and placed it on the table. "It's at two o'clock."

"Thank you for this," Emily said. "You seem to know how to be helpful to someone who's blind."

"My late wife's father was blind," he replied.

"I'm so sorry for your loss."

"Thank you," he said. "We have a nine-year-old daughter. She's kept me going."

Emily's chin came up. "I have a nine-year-old, too. She's my ward, actually. I became her legal guardian when her grandmother died recently."

"Wow," Grant replied. "That's a kind thing for you to do."

"Zoe came into my life less than two years ago," Emily said. Her voice became heavy with emotion. "She's been incredibly helpful to me in adjusting to my blindness. In many ways, she's kept me going, too."

"Care and concern for other people are crucial in a crisis. My aunt—this is her house—helped with Diedre after her mom died and made us home-cooked meals for a year."

"I met your aunt briefly when I arrived. She seems like a real powerhouse of a person."

Grant chuckled. "That she is. Take this house, for example. She's overseen its restoration." He cleared his throat, warming to the subject. "It's one of the most prominent examples of Georgian architecture ..."

My eyes began to droop as he rattled on about columns and cornices. Judging from Emily's animated responses and questions, she was quite interested in what Grant had to say. I was not. I sank to the floor, turned on my side, and gave in to sleep.

I woke to the sounds of music with a heavy drumbeat coming from the backyard. The voices of the partygoers rose with the level of the music.

"The entertainment has started," Grant said. "Would you like to dance?"

Emily shook her head. "I'm still getting used to being in crowds," she said. "I've loved talking to you. Thank you for bringing me dinner. The food was delicious. I hope you don't think I'm rude, but I'd like to find your aunt and say goodbyes."

"I know my aunt," he said, getting to his feet. "She'll have dragged my uncle onto the dance floor. Craig and Gina will be there, as well. How are you getting home?"

"I'll call a rideshare."

"Why don't you dial it up? I'll walk you out and wait with you until it gets here. Then I can come back inside and make your excuses for you."

"You wouldn't mind?"

"Not at all."

Emily ordered her ride. The voice-over announced it would be there in ten minutes.

We followed Grant out the front door and onto the lawn. They stood next to each other, facing the street. Emily released my harness and held me by my leash.

"I think I may sneak out early, too," Grant said. "My daughter is starting at a new school in the city on Monday. We're going shopping for a new outfit tomorrow. I think I'm going to need all the strength I can get for that errand."

"Which school?" Emily asked.

Grant supplied the name of the school.

Emily threw her head back and laughed. "What a coincidence! Zoe is starting there—in fourth grade—a week from Monday. I wonder if they'll be in the same class."

He'd turned to her.

"Do you and your husband live near there?"

"I'm ... we're getting a divorce," Emily said.

Grant stood close to her. I looked between the two of them. I'd seen those same expressions on the faces of couples in the Disney movies we watched with Zoe.

A lightbulb went off in my head.

I rose to my feet and began to walk around them.

Neither of them noticed me. Emily and Grant continued to talk about the new school.

I walked around and around, circling them with my leash until they had to step toward each other.

Emily stumbled into Grant, resting her hands on his chest. "Garth," she said. "What in the world?"

Grant put his arms around her to steady her. "Good boy, Garth," he said. "I think he's got the right idea." He touched her cheek, then lowered his face to hers and kissed her softly.

I turned my head away to give them some privacy and my gaze fell upon my most favorite food in the whole wide world. There, at the base of the stand where the valet stored car keys, lay an unmistakable orange cylinder.

Our car arrived, and Emily and Grant pulled apart.

"May I call you?" Grant asked breathlessly.

"I'd like that," Emily said. She gave him her number.

He put his hand on the small of her back and guided her to the car.

I was able to swerve to my right just enough to clean up the Crunchy Cheeto that was littering the lawn. I know it's against guide dog protocol, but I always like to be helpful.

THANK YOU FOR READING!

If you enjoyed *The Unexpected Path*, I'd be
grateful if you wrote a review.

Just a few lines would be great. Reviews on Goodreads and
Amazon are the best gift an author can receive. They encourage
us when they're good, help us improve our next book when
they're not, and help other readers make informed choices
when purchasing books. Reviews keep the Amazon algorithms
humming and are the most helpful aide in selling books!

To post a review on Amazon or for Kindle:

1. Go to the product detail page for *The Unexpected
   Path* at
2. Amazon.com.
3. Click "Write a customer review" in the Customer
   Reviews section.
4. Write your review and click Submit.

In gratitude,
Barbara Hinske

BOOK CLUB QUESTIONS

1. Do you personally know anyone who is blind?
2. If so, what is your observation of their ability to live a normal life?
3. Have you observed anyone using a screen reader?
4. What is your personal reaction when you encounter a visually impaired person? Do you offer to help or stay out of their way?
5. The newly blind find going out terrifying and may self-isolate. Can you relate to this?
6. Have you had to cope with a life-altering disability for yourself or a family member?
7. How did you feel about Emily and Gina's attempts to patch up their friendship?
8. Visually impaired people report that they all occasionally get lost. Have you ever gotten lost? How did the experience make you feel?
9. Do you know any service dogs?

10. Can you understand how service dogs bring the blind out of self-imposed isolation and provide the comfort and love that all pets do?

ACKNOWLEDGMENTS

I'm blessed with the wisdom and support of many kind and generous people. I want to thank the most supportive and delightful group of champions an author could hope for:

Steve Pawlowski for starting me on this most gratifying path;

My insightful and supportive assistant Lisa Coleman who keeps all the plates spinning;

My life coach Mat Boggs for your wisdom and guidance;

My kind and generous legal team, Kenneth Kleinberg, Esq., and Michael McCarthy—thank you for believing in my vision;

The professional "dream team" of my editors Linden Gross, Jesika St. Clair, and proofreader Dana Lee; and

Elizabeth Mackey for a beautiful, poignant cover.

ABOUT THE AUTHOR

USA Today Bestselling Author BARBARA HINSKE is an attorney and novelist. She's authored the Guiding Emily series, the mystery thriller collection "Who's There?", the Paws & Pastries series, two novellas in The Wishing Tree series, and the beloved *Rosemont Series*. Her novella *The Christmas Club* was made into a Hallmark Channel movie of the same name in 2019.

She is extremely grateful to her readers! She inherited the writing gene from her father who wrote mysteries when he retired and told her a story every night of her childhood. She and her husband share their own Rosemont with two adorable and spoiled dogs. The old house keeps her husband busy with repair projects and her happily decorating, entertaining, and gardening. She also spends a lot of time baking and—as a result —dieting.

PLEASE ENJOY THE FIRST CHAPTER OF OVER EVERY HURDLE, BOOK 3 IN THE GUIDING EMILY SERIES

Over Every Hurdle

Chapter 1

Emily Main lifted a handful of her heavy auburn hair with one hand and fanned the damp nape of her neck with the other. "What do you think? Does the buffet look pretty? I want everything to be perfect. It needs to be elegant and classy for Gina."

Martha Main put her arm around her daughter's shoulders and gave them a squeeze. "It's absolutely gorgeous. The tea sandwiches you girls made this morning look fantastic. So dainty."

"I cut off all the crusts," Zoe chimed in, proud of her contribution. The fourth grader had recently become Emily's ward when her grandmother had died.

"You did a very precise job of it," Martha told the girl, whom she loved like a granddaughter. She turned to Emily, "The pastries you got from the bakery on the corner are stunning. They're little works of art."

"Thank you for making the scones, Mom. Yours are better than any I've had in a tearoom."

"I'm delighted I could contribute something to Gina's bridal shower," Martha replied. "I'm so happy she's marrying such a nice man. And I'm overjoyed that the two of you have rekindled your friendship."

Emily inhaled deeply. The rift between her and her lifelong best friend had been a painful chapter in her life. One she was thankful was finally over. "Did you put the flowers on the end table?" she asked Zoe.

"Yep. They're next to the sign that says 'Gifts.' Everything's set up like the map we made. Do you want me to lead you around the room so you can check everything?"

Emily shook her head. "That's not necessary. If you say it's all right, then it is. You're very reliable, Zoe—way more dependable than I was at your age." She wished she could see Zoe's reaction to her words, but Zoe's quick intake of breath told Emily that Zoe appreciated the compliment.

"How long before people start arriving?" Emily asked.

Martha consulted her watch. "Any minute now. Are you still expecting seven, including Gina?"

"Yes. It's a family shower. I hope Gina isn't disappointed. I didn't think I could manage—"

"Gina's thrilled you're doing this for her. I talked to her mother yesterday. Gina will have time to relax and talk to everyone. Her mother told me she's really looking forward to this afternoon."

Emily nodded. "Good. And Garth is in his bed? He's not working as my guide dog during the shower."

"He's stretched out and sound asleep," Zoe said. "Sabrina's cuddled up next to him."

"Okay. We don't want them getting under anyone's feet. It's your job to make sure Sabrina stays out of the way, Zoe."

"I know," Zoe said, a hint of rebuke in her voice.

Martha rubbed the girl's back in a circular motion. "It's always a bit nerve-wracking for the host right before a party starts. You keep going over the details in your mind to make sure you haven't forgotten anything."

"Let's put hot water into the teapots to warm them," Emily said. "There should be ten of them. Everyone can select their own tea from the box. We have twenty different varieties. It came in handy that you're such a big tea drinker, Mom."

Martha moved to the kitchen island and began filling the individual teapots with hot water from the large electric urn. "I had so much fun shopping for the teas for this shower. I also bought enough new kinds to try at home that I won't run out for at least a year."

"Thank you for letting me borrow teapots from your collection," Emily said.

"They're all so pretty," Zoe chimed in.

"I'm happy that they're getting pressed into service," Martha said. "I love them, but I rarely use them. I just plop a tea bag into a mug at home."

"If I drank tea every day and had a teapot, I'd use it," Zoe said.

"Quite right. Is one of these your favorite?" Martha asked.

Zoe walked to the kitchen island and stood, surveying the ten teapots lined up in two rows. "It's a tie between the one with yellow daisies that are sort of raised up on the sides and the one that's a shiny bright blue."

"You've got a good eye," Martha said. "The one with the

daisies is handmade. My husband got it for me in Sausalito for our first anniversary. It's my favorite. The other one is Fiestaware."

"I'll tell you what—let's put both of these aside so that Zoe can have the blue one for her teapot and you can have the one Dad gave you for yours, Mom."

"Can we?" Zoe asked.

"Of course," Emily said as the buzzer from the lobby sounded. She made her way to the door and pressed the button to open the lobby door. "I think our first guests are here. Go do that quickly, Zoe. It's showtime!"

Gina Roberts and her mother swept into Emily's apartment. "Are we the first to arrive?" Gina asked as she drew Emily into a hug. "It's poor form for the bride to be late."

"Mom and Zoe are here, of course," Emily said. "But no one else."

"Good. We had a heck of a time finding a parking spot. Drove around the block twice." Hilary Roberts, Gina's mother, walked up to Emily and took both of her hands in hers. "Hello, dear girl. I..." her voice broke. "This is the first time I've seen you since..." She drew in a deep breath.

"Since I lost my eyesight," Emily finished her sentence for her. "I know. You've been on your retirement round-the-world tour. How was it?"

Hilary cleared her throat. "It was wonderful—mostly. We saw everything on our bucket list and decided on a few places we'd like to go back to, but being away for over a year was too much for me. If it hadn't been for Charles, I would have bolted for home months ahead of schedule."

"I was proud of you for stepping out of your comfort zone and going," Emily said. "I'd love to hear more about your favorite experiences during tea."

"I'll sit with you this afternoon and do just that." Hilary stepped back, holding Emily at arm's length. "You look terrific, Em. You've always been beautiful, and you're still full of the self-confidence, poise, and presence you've always had." They remained silent. "I'm so glad."

"Thank you," Emily said quietly. "The past couple of years have been rough, but Mom's been a rock star this whole time and I've been blessed with the most supportive co-workers you could ever hope for—not to mention Gina. The training I've received from the Foundation for the Blind has allowed me to resume my independent life, and having Garth at my side," she gestured to where her guide dog lay on his bed in a corner of the room, "is... well... everything."

"Gina told me you have a remarkable guide dog," Hilary said. "There are two dogs over there."

"The schnauzer is mine," Zoe said. "She's not trained to be a guide dog, but she's really smart—just like Garth."

"You must be Zoe," Hilary said, turning to the girl. She extended her hand; Zoe took it and they shook. "I'm Gina's mom. You can call me Hilary. My daughter thinks the world of you. She says you've been extremely helpful to Emily—and that you've been through a lot, too."

Zoe sidled over to Emily.

"I was so sorry to hear about your grandmother. I knew Irene and liked her very much."

Zoe swallowed hard, and Emily put her arm around the little girl's shoulders.

"That's a very pretty dress you're wearing, Zoe," Gina broke in. "The yellow is beautiful with your dark hair and eyes. Vibrant. It suits you."

Martha caught Zoe's eye and winked at her.

Zoe flushed. "I love this color."

The buzzer sounded again, and Emily moved toward the sound. She pressed the button to open the lobby door. "We're going to have tea as soon as everyone arrives. Then we'll open gifts."

"Did you receive mine?" Hilary asked. "I had the store send it here."

Emily nodded. "It's in my bedroom. Zoe—can you get the wrapped package that's sitting on top of the dresser and put it on the gifts table?"

Zoe took off to retrieve Hilary's gift as Emily buzzed in another guest and opened her door.

"Emily," called a vaguely familiar voice. "I'm Craig's aunt. We met at the engagement party I threw for Craig and Gina."

"Yes—I remember. It was a..." She paused, searching for the right words. She'd spent the entire party secluded in the library of the palatial Georgian home, avoiding the boisterous party while getting to know Craig's twin brother, Grant Johnson. Not only getting to know him, but becoming romantically interested in him.

"Grant can't stop talking about you," the woman behind Grant's aunt chimed in. "Sylvia Johnson," said the woman, taking Emily's hand in hers. "I'm Craig and Grant's mother. I'm pleased to meet you. Thank you so much for inviting me."

Emily and Sylvia shook hands warmly. Emily could feel a flush rise up from the open neckline of her floral-patterned dress. She and Grant had spoken on the phone almost every night since they'd met but had only found time to see each other twice—once for dinner and another time for a midweek cup of coffee. His busy schedule as an architect and widowed father, together with her demanding job and new responsibilities with Zoe, allowed scant time for their budding relationship. She was pleased that he'd spoken about her to his mother.

"Please… come in," Emily said, stepping aside.

"I want to introduce you to someone else," Sylvia said. "I hope you don't mind that we brought her along. Meet Diedre—Grant's daughter."

"Hi Diedre! Your dad's told me so much about you." Emily spoke into the space in front of her. "I'm glad you decided to come, after all."

"I talked her into it," Gina said. "I told her that there'd be another girl here her age, so it would be fun for her. I figured you'd have more than enough food."

"Of course," Emily said. "As a matter of fact, I think both you and Zoe are new fourth graders at Hillside Elementary. I don't believe you're in the same class, but maybe you've seen each other."

Diedre shrugged and stared at the floor.

Sylvia bent over and spoke softly into Diedre's ear. "Emily is like your other grandfather. She can't see, so you have to talk to her."

The buzzer sounded again.

"That'll be my three cousins," Gina said. "They were driving into San Francisco together. We're all here! Let's get this party started."

From *Over Every Hurdle*

ALSO BY BARBARA HINSKE

Available at Amazon in Print, Audio, and for Kindle

The Rosemont Series

Coming to Rosemont

Weaving the Strands

Uncovering Secrets

Drawing Close

Bringing Them Home

Shelving Doubts

Restoring What Was Lost

No Matter How Far

When Dreams There Be

Novellas

The Night Train

The Christmas Club (adapted

for The Hallmark Channel, 2019)

Paws & Pastries

Sweets & Treats

Snowflakes, Cupcakes & Kittens (coming 2023)

Workout Wishes & Valentine Kisses

Wishes of Home

Novels in the Guiding Emily Series

Guiding Emily

The Unexpected Path

Over Every Hurdle

Down the Aisle

Novels in the "Who's There?!" Collection

Deadly Parcel

Final Circuit

CONNECT WITH BARBARA
HINSKE ONLINE

Sign up for her newsletter at **BarbaraHinske.com**
    Goodreads.com/BarbaraHinske
    Facebook.com/BHinske
    Instagram/barbarahinskeauthor
    TikTok.com/BarbaraHinske
    Pinterest.com/BarbaraHinske
    Twitter.com/BarbaraHinske
    Search for **Barbara Hinske on YouTub**e
    bhinske@gmail.com

Made in United States
Orlando, FL
05 January 2024

42055094R00188